Touched by an Angel

VICTORIA CHRISTOPHER MURRAY

With

PRINCESS F.L. GOODEN

D1534254

Houston, Texas * Washington, D.C.

Touched by an Angel © 2014 by Victoria Christopher Murray
with Princess F.L. Gooden

Brown Girls Publishing, LLC
www.browngirlspublishing.com

ISBN:
9781625177087 eISBN
9781625177094 print ISBN

First Brown Girls Publishing LLC trade printing

Manufactured and Printed in the United States of America

Acknowledgments
Princess

I know GOD made this possible, and I can't thank Him enough. Thank you for this gift and for sending someone to teach me how to use it.

To Victoria, because of you I have experienced being "touched by an angel." I will never be the same again. I prayed a small prayer to God and He led me to you. You give it to me straight and I am grateful for that. I am also grateful for your patience and faith in me. I still think this a dream.

To my husband, Reginald, thank you. You played every role I needed to get to this point. My listening ear, my coach, my drill sergeant, friend, shoulder....just everything. I thank God for you!

To my mother, this is our first step toward the penthouse. We will get there. One book down... many to come.

To the children (my role models), Aiyana, Briana, Chris, Zahna, Peyton, and Kelsey, thank you all for not only telling me but showing me what to do in order to achieve my dreams. Quitting is never an option with you guys. I am very proud of all of you. To Rebecca Gentry, you know why... I love and thank you! To my brother Eric, sister Nichole, Des, and Jas – my "Ride or Die Crew" this is only the beginning. Thank you all for always being there. To my brother Pastor

C.D., you don't say a whole lot but you pray and that is what I will always need. Thank you! To my sister Paige, my next book will be about "your" daddy. It will become a movie because drama sells. Then we can take some of the money and have Jay build us twin cars that no one will have but us. Thank you both for listening to my stories when you were babies. It's good if you don't remember some of them. To my entire family and everyone else reading this—I am grateful for all of your love and support. I don't want to leave anyone out.

And one more thing, to Victoria and ReShonda—you all didn't just change the game. . . you changed my life. I will be forever grateful. Thank you!

A Note from
Victoria

Writing is in my blood. Writing good stories is who I am. And nothing gives me joy like being able to nurture and develop new talent.

When I started Brown Girls Publishing along with ReShonda Tate Billingsley, our goal was to give fan favorites and fresh voices a chance to bring their stories to the masses. We discovered so many talented writers, many with stories waiting to share with the world. The teacher in me, the part that loves nurturing and developing up and coming writers, now had a plethora of material to choose from. As I continued working with some of those writers, there are a few who stood out from the crowd, who I truly wanted to take under my literary wings and watch them soar.

I am happy to present to you one of those writers.

Princess F.L. Gooden is the first fresh voice that Brown Girls is presenting as part of our mentoring partnership. It was amazing to watch her growth as we wrote this book together. I can't wait to see where she goes from here!

Hope you enjoy OUR story! More to come, so stay tuned!

Victoria

Touched
by an
Angel

Chapter
ONE

With the bare tips of my fingers, I lifted the red thong from my husband's suitcase, slowly, deliberately as if it were a pit viper. My lips parted into a wide O as I stared at the lace underwear, panties that I'd never seen before.

It wasn't like I was searching for trouble; in the twenty-three years of my marriage to Sheldon, there had never been anything close to drama in our relationship, especially not this kind. The two of us were solid, the kind of couple that Ashford and Simpson sang about back in the day when as a teenager, I dreamed about the man who would take my hand after my father walked me down the aisle. That man had been Sheldon Hudson—and he'd kept every single one of the vows we'd shared on our wedding day.

At least that's what I'd always thought.

I took a deep breath, just to make sure that I was still alive.

Why am I still holding onto these? I wondered.

But even as I had that thought, I could not release the death grip the tips of my fingers had on the panties. In my mind, I imagined the woman who owned this strip of material and I could almost see myself—twenty years younger. I could hear myself—with a high-pitched tone that belonged to someone who had not yet fully stepped into womanhood. And worse—I could see Sheldon—grinning as the tramp sauntered toward him wearing nothing more than these five inches of silk and lace. And maybe a pair of matching stilettos.

I snatched myself from that nightmare and shook my head. How in the world had I ended up here? After all, it wasn't like I was sneaking around, rummaging through my husband's bag as if I was a wife with no trust. No, I was doing what I'd always done when Sheldon returned home from a business trip.

Like all the other times, the car service had dropped him off in front of the house less than an hour ago and he had dragged himself and his bag across the trace of snow that sprinkled the path to the front door of our Capitol Hill townhouse. His eyes were blood-shot with exhaustion from the red-eye flight he'd taken from Los Angeles.

But even though he was tired, he'd kissed me with every bit of energy he had left and I followed him as he dragged his suitcase up the spiral staircase to the second level of our home.

Inside our master suite, Sheldon had dropped his luggage at the foot of our bed, tossed his briefcase and cell phone onto the bed, then staggered into the bathroom.

While he relaxed under the double heads in our steam shower, I had eagerly unzipped his bag in search of my gift. Years ago, he'd given up hiding my surprise—now, he laid it on top for me to uncover quickly. From perfume to pearls, he always brought home something that put a smile on my face and gratitude in my heart. And today, just days away from Christmas, I couldn't imagine what I would find.

And...well, I had never expected to find this!

The sound of the shower shutting off, snapped me from my shock and my head twisted toward the bathroom. Through the closed door, I heard Sheldon singing his favorite song.

I believe in you and me...

I believe that we will be...

In love eternally...

When the movie, *The Preacher's Wife* had hit the big screen, Sheldon had declared that this song was our song.

As he sang, I could tell he was rejuvenated and refreshed; inside the richness of his tenor, I heard his anticipation.

I did the only thing I could—I stood still and waited until the door opened and Sheldon stepped out. His damp skin glistened and his smile was just as bright. The towel tucked at his waist was loose as if he didn't plan for it to stay there long.

"Hey, baby." His greeting was filled with the lust that always came from being away from home for five days.

Still grasping it with just my fingertips, I held up the thong. "What is this?" I asked. I didn't even recognize my own voice—my tone was as deep as my husband's.

His smile rolled upside down and he squinted, trying to see what I held. "What's what?"

My heart pounded with a pain that made me want to fall to my knees. But, I pressed through it and held the underwear higher—straight in front of his face for his eyes to see what mine had seen.

His frown deepened. "What's that?" he asked again as if he didn't know.

I had hoped for more from the man who had promised that he would forsake all others. I had expected my upstanding husband to confess right away that he'd fallen and quickly beg for my forgiveness. Maybe then, there would have been a slither of a chance that I would forgive him and we could somehow find a way to move on.

But now, there was no chance of reconciliation. Not if he was going to play me like this. Not if he was going to lie and deny.

The words of my three-time-divorced best friend came to me now.

"Men cheat, and then they lie. That's what 'man' stands for—men-admit-nothing."

Theresa had lost her faith in men a long time ago, even though I constantly worked to get her to see that all men weren't the same. And, I always held up Sheldon as Exhibit One. But now it seemed like Theresa was the one who needed to be schooling me.

"Savannah, sweetheart." His voice was full of the same confusion that was etched deep in the lines on his face. "What *is* that? Why are you showing me those..."

"Don't you dare do that, Sheldon," my voice quivered as I interrupted him. "Don't you dare stand there and tell me that you have no idea what these are." I shook the cloth between my fingertips.

"I don't."

Raising my hand high, I tossed the satin and lace toward him; the thong hung for a moment in the air before landing at his toes. "Whose are those?" I screamed. "Who do those panties belong to?"

He held up his hands, shook his head. "I don't know what you're talking about."

"I'm talking about you bringing your whore's underwear into my home."

"What?" Now, his voice was as loud as mine.

"I'm talking about you cheating on me. How could you do this?" I cried.

"I don't know what..."

I didn't let him finish. "Don't deny it, Sheldon!" I screamed. "I found those in your bag; I'm not stupid, I know what those panties mean."

Now, he said nothing. And, it was the way he stood silent that made me snap. That made me rush to him with my fingers clutched into fists, ready to attack. But he grabbed my wrists before I could begin my assault.

"I can't believe you did this to me!" I said. "After all these years. After all the love that I've given to you. After *everything* that I've given to you." Fury gave me the strength to wrestle free from his grasp and I pounded my fists against his chest.

His eyes widened at my punches and he tried to push me away.

Stammering, he began, "I...I...I..."

The beginning of his confession came out in a gurgle. "I...," he said again before his legs shook, his knees bowed, he fell to the floor, the towel now completely free.

I stood there for a moment, confused. Was this really the way Sheldon was going to handle this? He was going to pretend that he fainted?

But then, it was the way he laid there, his eyes rolled back, his fingers clutching the skin on his chest.

Now, it was my eyes that widened and I dropped to the floor.

"Sheldon!" I sounded different now. Yes, I shouted, but my voice was filled with panic.

His mouth opened and his eyelids closed.

"Sheldon!" I pressed my fingertips against his neck, felt his pulse, then jumped from his side. Rushing to the nightstand, I grabbed the telephone.

"Help me, please," I exclaimed to the 9-1-1 operator. "My husband. He collapsed. I think he's had a heart attack!"

Chapter
TWO

We lived on Capitol Hill—home to Congressional leaders and legislative aides. So, I knew it wasn't going to take long for the EMTs to arrive.

"Please, Sheldon. Please, hold on."

His eyes would open, not even an eighth of an inch, but then, they would close again as if he needed even that energy to struggle for every breath.

"Please, Sheldon," I begged him over and over as my tears watered his chest. "Hold on."

The moment I heard the sirens, I released my husband and dashed to the stairs. All the way down, I prayed that Sheldon would still be alive when I came back up. Because what would I do if he died?

I opened the door and the EMTs rushed in, bringing a gust of December's frigid wind with them.

"Up there." I pointed and then, I led the way.

In our bedroom, I stood back, watched my husband, and listened to the medical men speak a language that I didn't understand. And, I cried.

What had I done? But then, even in the midst of my fear, I still wondered, what had Sheldon done?

Within minutes, the men had Sheldon on a gurney and as the two of them carried him from the bedroom, I grabbed my cell and purse and threw the first coat that I could snatch over my sweat pants and T-shirt.

Outside, they rolled Sheldon into the emergency vehicle, then, one helped me to step up and climb into the cramped and crowded space.

"Where are we going?" I asked as the ambulance sped away from our home.

"Howard University Hospital." The paramedic didn't look up from whatever he was tapping into a tablet.

The other man was right next to Sheldon wiring him up, and doing other things that I didn't understand, but knew were saving his life.

I wanted to ask questions, the primary one being, would my husband live? But I said nothing, needing the men who were fighting to save Sheldon's life to stay focused.

All I wanted to do was to be right by Sheldon's side, but there almost wasn't even enough room to breathe in the small space, so I just wrapped my arms around myself, bowed my head and prayed...*Please, God. Please, God. Please, God.*

My eyes were closed as I heard, "Blood pressure's one-sixty over one-hundred."

I'd seen the walkie-talkie in the paramedic's hand, so I knew he was speaking to someone at the hospital.

He continued, "He's breathing, but not responding at this time. It appears to be a heart attack."

"What's your ETA?" the emergency room dispatcher's voice crackled through the machine.

"Five minutes."

"Copy that," she responded before signing out.

Then, I heard the voice of the other paramedic.

"Sir, can you hear me?"

Nothing from my husband.

"Hang in there," the EMT worker encouraged. "We'll get you to ER as fast as we can."

I lifted my head from my prayer and my eyes rested on Sheldon. I stared at the man whom I'd loved with everything inside of me for so many years and I felt nothing but a clash of emotions.

My husband was laying there, I was sure, fighting for his life. And that scared me.

But then, the other side of my heart beat with anger, making my mind race back to the moments before he collapsed.

This really was...convenient was the only word that I could come up with. Lying there, he didn't have to answer any questions. Lying there, he didn't have to confess.

Just a moment ago, I was praying for him, but now, I wanted to grab him and shake him until all of his secrets loosened and fell from their hiding places.

My mind was boggled with questions. How could Sheldon not know whose thong was in his suitcase?

His! Suitcase!

And why would he deny it? Did he really believe that I would fall for his lies? Why didn't he just tell me the truth since the evidence hung from my fingertips?

That was what had me so fired up with fury. He'd cheated; that broke my heart. But then, he lied. And that shredded what was left of my heart into nothing.

He should have had enough respect and love for me that once he was caught, he confessed.

If he had told me everything: who she was, how many times, when and where. And why...then, maybe we wouldn't be here now. Maybe we'd be at home trying to work it out.

"Does he have a history of heart issues, high blood pressure, seizures, anything?"

It wasn't until I blinked a few times, that I realized the paramedic was talking to me.

"What?"

He repeated the question.

"You want to know his history?" I asked. "I'm not sure of his history," I snapped. "People keep secrets. They tell you only what they want you to know."

It was the way both men looked at me that made me regret my words. I didn't sound like the loving wife who feared losing her husband.

But the truth was, I did love Sheldon. I had loved this man for more than half of the years of my life and I wouldn't know how to live if Sheldon died. Especially since, I'd never be able to forget that I was pounding on his chest right before he collapsed.

If he left me now, all I'd have would be a guilty conscience, a torn heart, a red thong, and no answers.

I wouldn't be able to live with that, so I sucked back my anger, and kept my thoughts on my husband, whom I loved, rather than my husband, the cheat.

The paramedics didn't ask me another question and I hoped these men just took my words as a distressed wife who was terrified of losing her husband.

I wasn't close enough to Sheldon to touch him, but now that I had a new focus, I hoped that he'd be able to hear me. "Baby, please hang in there. I don't want to lose you."

That was the truth.

Finally, the ambulance pulled to a sudden stop and the doors to the vehicle swung open. The paramedics jumped out, moved to the side of the ambulance and gave information to someone who might have been a hospital administrator.

I took that time alone in the ambulance to move to Sheldon's side, and I stroked his arm. Maybe if he felt my touch, he'd want to come back. Or maybe, he'd just think it was...her.

I snatched my hand away from him.

"Ma'am, you can get out now."

I turned to a man wearing scrubs; he took my hand to help me climb out as others jumped into the ambulance. Seconds later, they had Sheldon lowered and wheeled into the hospital.

I had to trot to keep up with the medical team as they wheeled Sheldon first into an elevator then, down a hall on the third floor.

Again, I wanted to ask questions, but I didn't want to hinder anyone from doing this job perfectly.

Just as the gurney made a turn to the left, a nurse stepped aside and led me to the right.

"Where..." was all I could get out.

"We've prepared a room for your husband so that the doctors can evaluate him," she said as she led me into a waiting room. "Someone will be out as soon as they can to update you. In the meantime," she paused and handed me a clipboard from another nurse who stood at her side. I hadn't even seen the second woman. The nurse continued, "If you can fill out these forms, we'll have your husband taken care of."

Then, the two scurried away, giving me no chance to say another word.

I felt like she'd left me alone, even though I wasn't. This was Howard University, in the middle of Washington DC. A Saturday morning, five days before Christmas.

So, the waiting room was packed, almost every chair was taken. But I found a single seat beneath the television that hung high in one corner.

I didn't make eye contact with anyone, though I wasn't sure that I would've been able to even if that's what I wanted. Every eye in the room was plastered to the television and a quick glance told me it was one of those housewives shows—either that or a boxing match; I could never tell the difference.

I sat in that only vacant chair and sighed. I needed to fill out these forms, but first, I needed for my hands to stop shaking. As I laid the clipboard onto the table next to me, I stared down at the model who was staring back from the cover of *Elle* Magazine.

The chestnut colored woman was tall, beyond thin, with hair so voluminous it covered half of her body. With her fake boobs, itty-bitty waist and legs that were too long for the magazine's cover to show, she was so beautiful. Just the type of woman who would wear a red thong.

I turned that magazine cover over only to see another. This time Beyoncé and Jay Z graced that spot. But even though the photo showed the couple black-tie glamorous, holding hands as they exited some soiree, the headline above their picture screamed: HOW MANY AFFAIRS HAS JAY Z HAD?

If I'd been alone, I would have thrown that magazine across the room. Instead, I just turned it over, gave up on the magazines, and leaned back, even though I wanted to jump up and run through the hospital's halls until someone told me something about my husband.

I wrapped the strap of my purse around my arm twice, then closed my eyes. I needed to rest, even if it were for a second. I needed my mind to have just a moment of peace.

But even with deep breaths that I'd learned in my yoga classes, my mind raced with the same question—how could Sheldon have done this to me?

There was just no way for me to make sense of this.

Yes, I knew that many (including my best friend) believed that all men cheated. But whenever I heard that line, inside, I always said, *not my husband*. Not Sheldon Hudson.

It was more than the fact that our love for each other went way down to our souls. It was in the way Sheldon loved me, the way he told me, the way he showed me.

And our sex life? It was as great as it had ever been.

"I can't stand being away from you," he had said just about every time he left for one of his business trips to Los Angeles.

And then he came back, always hungry, always thirsty for me. At home, we were the hero and heroine in the world's best romance novel, always touching, always feeling.

We had an always kind of love.

But right when I was settling into those memories, my eyes popped open as I remembered something else. Of our anniversary, back in August....

I pushed the tray to the side, then stretched out in the bed, completely satisfied.

A moment later, Sheldon strutted back into our bedroom, his arms filled with dozens of red roses.

"First pancakes and eggs and turkey bacon in bed and now this?" I said as he handed me the flowers.

I inhaled the fragrance of his love as he kissed my forehead. "There is nothing too good for my queen."

His words were simple. His words made me tingle.

He took the flowers from my arms, then held my hands in his. "For our anniversary celebration tonight, I want to try something a little different."

I tilted my head to the side, not understanding. "Different?"

"Yes." His grin was so wide, I thought he would bust. "I really wanted this to be a surprise, but I decided that I needed to let you know so you'll be prepared."

Then, he stood and handed me my robe.

"Where are we going?" I asked as I secured the belt around my waist.

He wouldn't say a word, though. He just held my hand, led me down the stairs, and onto the deck in the back of our townhouse. A tent covered half of the space.

"What's this?" I asked, thinking that it looked like the kind of camp-out gear that he used for our children back in the day. When they wanted to pretend that they were sleeping out in the woods—in the middle of Washington, DC.

"This is where I want us to celebrate twenty-three wonderful years of marriage."

I frowned, but he didn't seem to notice.

"Tonight, I want us to get dressed up, and then, we'll have dinner, catered of course, out here. And then," he wrapped his arms around me, "we'll make amazing love under the stars for God to see."

Gently, I pushed away from him. "For God and all the world to see," I said, looking to the left and then to the right. Both of our neighbors' patios were just feet away.

Had Sheldon forgotten where we lived? In the heart of downtown? The houses were so close together that if we made love out here, even the President and his wife would hear us in the White House.

"Baby, don't worry, this tent was just so I could show you what I had in mind. The one that I've ordered, no one will see, no one will hear."

As much as I always wanted to do whatever my husband wanted, this was one request that I would never be able to grant.

Making love outside, and not inside? Sure, he'd have some kind of bedding out here, but it wouldn't be a bed.

I shook my head thinking about how uncomfortable it would be. "This doesn't feel very romantic to me," I told him.

The grin that he'd worn, the one that had him looking like he would burst, faded fast, leaving the corners of his lips drooping.

Taking his hands, I said, "All I want to do tonight is go to that new restaurant on Fourteenth Street. And then we can stroll around U Street just like always. You know that's one of my favorite things to do." Then, trying to give him his smile back, I added, "And after that, we can come home and you can do wonderful things to me."

After a moment, he pulled me into his arms, then gave me a peck on my lips. "If that's what you want...."

"I do."

"Then, I'll make it happen. Because you mean everything to me."

And that's what he'd done. He'd shown me how much he loved me, by giving me what I wanted. Sheldon had gotten us into that chic new restaurant that only served twenty couples a night, and had a three-week waiting list.

It had been a wonderful anniversary for me: dinner with the man I loved, and then making love at home. Of course, it had been the same—missionary style, in our bed. But that was what was most familiar. But maybe familiar wasn't so good anymore.

Thinking about it now, Sheldon had met my needs, but had I met his? That night, I'd not only thrown a wrench into his plans, I'd dumped the entire toolbox out on him.

Maybe that was it, maybe Sheldon was bored with me, with us. Maybe that's what the red-thonged, gorgeous, younger, definitely-a-model-type girl gave him. Maybe she was free, maybe she was a freak.

And I was sure that she definitely wasn't a good girl, the kind of girl I'd been my whole life.

My eyes were open, but it wasn't hard to imagine her. I could see Sheldon's woman with her flat stomach and legs so long they wrapped around his back—twice. She was the kind of women who knew how to make all kinds of fantasies come true. She probably had green eyes, like that model on the magazine cover and she made Sheldon forget that he had a wife at home who no longer had a flat stomach because of the two big babies she'd birthed—at the same time. He'd forgotten that he had a wife whose hips had spread and thighs had expanded because that's what happened when you kept living.

He had traded me in for a younger, newer model.

In my head, all kinds of thoughts whirled, all kinds of images swirled until a volcano of emotions exploded inside of me.

I was going to kill him!

The moment I had that thought, my eyes rested on the table on the other side of me.

And, I saw the Bible.

My aching heart was convicted. How could I talk about killing a man who may very well be dying?

It was definitely time for me to pray again.

So as the TV above me blasted, a newscaster from CNN began explaining the gory details of a woman that was murdered because of a love triangle, I quickly bowed my head and spoke loudly in my head.

"Dear God, please forgive me. I don't want Sheldon to die; I don't even really want to kill him. Well, maybe a little...." But then, I rushed to say, "No, I wouldn't. It's just that, God...I'm so scared, and confused, and mad...all at the same time. I don't know what to feel. I don't know what to do.

"So, I'm going to do what You would want me to do. I'm asking You to heal, Sheldon. Heal him completely and fully." I paused, not sure where I should go from there.

And then, I felt a small voice: *Pray for what you want.*

"I want to kill him, Lord!" And then, I asked for forgiveness because I wasn't playing when I said that. But then, I added, "After I kill him, I think I want my marriage, too, Lord. I'm not trying to be double-minded or unsure; I'm just confused.

"But I do know that You chose Sheldon for me. I'm sure of that. So I'm praying for revelation. Please reveal what I need to know about this situation, and then, heal my marriage. Because You said in Your word that whatever You put together, no man or skank-a-rella could ever take away."

She paused. "I know that's not completely Biblical, Father, but you know what I mean, right?"

It wasn't until I opened my eyes and a tear dripped onto my hand, that I realized I was crying again.

This was a roller coaster of emotions. But if anyone would get me through this, it would be God.

Chapter
THREE

On the twelfth day of Christmas my true love gave to me....
I wondered who I could talk to about turning down the Muzak that played above. It was soft, nothing more than background noise. But it blared in my ears. Maybe it was because every fifth song that played seemed to be this one, Sheldon's and my favorite.

Glancing down at my watch, I couldn't believe that it was just about noon. Had it only been four hours? Once again, I stood and peeked into the hallway, glancing at the women at the Nurses' station.

There was no doubt that they saw me; they knew I needed information. But I guess they had nothing to give. So with a sigh, I turned back into the room and strolled to the window.

Snow.

I didn't even know that it had begun to snow. Winter was definitely here, though not officially until tomorrow. Winter, Sheldon's favorite time of the year. He loved everything about the colder temperatures: sipping hot chocolate, cuddling with me on the sofa. We even roasted chestnuts on an open fire.

And then, I wondered...would Sheldon ever get to do any of those things again?

Turning around, I marched back toward the door. This time somebody was going to have to tell me something.

Before I stepped out of the room, though, the nurse who had first directed me into the waiting room, came in.

"Do you have news about my husband?" I asked before she could say anything to me.

She shook her head. "No, I was just checking on you. Is there anyone that I can call?"

Call? Call!

Oh, my God. I hadn't thought of that. "No, thank you," I said. "I'll call our children now." Then, again, I asked, "You don't know anything?"

To her, I probably sounded as if I didn't believe what she was saying. And really, I guess I didn't. She was a nurse; didn't nurses know everything?

But again, she shook her head and then, she turned away.

I wanted to go after her and demand a better answer. But, she had reminded me of what I couldn't believe that I'd forgotten. I'd been so consumed with double-minded thoughts—praying the Sheldon would make it, wishing that he and his red-thong lover would burn in the depths of....

I cleared my throat, hoping it would clear my mind as well. Right now, all I needed to think about were our children—Kym and Kyle. The twins needed to know what was going on now. Because, I wouldn't want the first call about Sheldon to be....

No! I wasn't going to think that way.

Reaching into my purse, I tilted it to one side and ended up with a handful of change and a peppermint.

Baby, if you put the change in your change purse, and your cell in the cell pocket, things would be a lot easier. You miss most of your calls digging into that dungeon that you call a purse.

Then, I heard his laugh and I shook his voice and his laughter from my head before I tilted my bag to the other side; my cell fell right into my hand.

I pulled it out, pressed the Home button, and right away, our children's faces popped up. Only this wasn't the photo that was on my phone; this was Sheldon's photo...Sheldon's phone!

I rewound it all in my mind. As I rushed from our home with the medics, I had picked up Sheldon's phone by accident. It was an easy mistake, a recurring mistake since we had the same phones, a two-for-one special that Sheldon couldn't pass up. We even had the same cases that he'd bought at a buy-one-get-one-free promotion.

It had never been any kind of issue before if we picked up each other's phones. But that was back when I was Sheldon's only woman.

I stared at my husband's phone and remembered my prayer. Well, I'd asked God to reveal what was going on. And here it was—a phone full of information and evidence.

Everything that I wanted to know was probably locked behind these keys. I was about to find out about the woman who caused Sheldon to risk twenty-three years of my love. I was about to learn what kind of *deal* she'd offered him.

Backing up, I fell into the chair where I'd been sitting, my eyes still focused on the phone.

Now that the evidence was in front of me, did I really want to know?

I nodded, told myself that I could do this, and ignored the twisting in my stomach. I hit the Home button again and Sheldon's picture of Kym and Kyle filled the screen once again.

"Where to start?"

Emails.

But I didn't have a name, so how was I supposed to find their salacious communications?

I opened up the email icon and scrolled through the first few: messages from me, from Kym, from Kyle, and then the others seemed to be all about business.

I sighed. This was going to take too long. So, I scrolled up to the search box and entered, 'I love you.'

Seconds later, several emails filled the screen: from me, from Kym, from Kyle. To me, to Kym, to Kyle.

Okay, that was too generic or they hadn't gotten to that level yet.

'Meet me,' was what I tried next.

Two emails popped up, both from Sheldon's business partner, Jon. At first, I sighed, but then, I clicked on one, and then the other because in today's times with all the down-low stuff...well, you know.

But then I felt ridiculous as my eyes scanned through the emails, the first one from Jon asking Sheldon how was the fundraiser in California, and the next one from Sheldon responding, raving about the success.

This was going nowhere, but I wasn't ready to give up.

'Can't wait to see you'—I tried that next.

My heart pounded when so many emails popped up this time. But as I searched through each...from Kym, from Kyle, to Kym, to Kyle. And there were at least a dozen 'I can't wait to see you' from Sheldon...to me.

I sighed. There was nothing here. Sheldon was far more duplicitous than I thought. His secrets were deeply hidden.

I didn't want to stop, though. I wanted to continue playing 'I Spy', but I had to call the children.

Then, I thought about Kym and how my drama queen would react. I couldn't call her just yet. I needed emotional support so that I could be strong for Kym and Kyle.

So instead of pressing the number for Kym, I punched in the telephone number for the person who would help me through this. The one who would soothe this all over for me, even though she was rough and tough and feisty.

The phone rang twice.

"Hola, Mr. Hudson. What's wrong?" she answered in a worry. I had forgotten that I'd given her Sheldon's number for emergency purposes.

"Hey, it's me."

Quickly her tone changed back to what I was use to. "Chica, I was just about to call and see if you wanted to grab lunch at Ohhh's and Ahhh's, but I said to myself, her man is home so, Resa, don't be no blocker."

Then my best friend filled the phone line with her hearty laughter, which was always so funny to me because I never could figure out how a woman who was barely five-two and weighed nothing but a minute could take up so much space the way Theresa did. And whenever she laughed, I laughed right along with her.

But today, my heart was too broken, and my head was packed with so much fear, that I couldn't even muster a smile.

Theresa Perez and I had been friends for almost thirty years, since our senior year of high school. She was a rough and tough New Yorker who'd moved to DC to live with her dad after she'd been expelled from her second high school in New York.

It wasn't that Theresa was a bad kid; it was that she didn't take no mess. From anyone.

And that was exactly the reason why we met.

As one of the All-Star Seniors, I had the privilege of working in the principal's office during my study period. It was one of the extracurricular activities that I'd been given because of my record: perfect grades—All As, perfect attendance—I never missed a day, not even if I had a cold, and I was the president of the Senior Class.

It was a Friday afternoon when my first period English teacher marched into the principal's office dragging this girl (who was mumbling in Spanish) behind her. Her clothes were in disarray—her blouse torn and the hem on her skirt was unraveling. But it was the massive mess of curls atop her head that told the tale. She'd been in a fight.

For a moment, I stood there shocked. What was this girl doing at this school anyway? She looked like she was in the seventh grade, eighth grade tops.

But then, Mrs. Wynn said, "Tell Mr. Bates that I need to speak to him about a student," and I knew this girl was a high schooler like me.

I tried to mind my business as my teacher and the girl went into the principal's office, but I couldn't help but hear the loud voice of the girl, speaking half-English, half-Spanish. I was studying French so I could only understand her English words, but I could tell that I was right, she'd been in a fight.

I was just about to leave the office for my next class when the principal's door finally swung open. Mrs. Wynn took two steps out, looked at me, and said, "I have an idea." She grabbed the girl's hand like she was a two-year-old and said, "Savannah, meet Theresa Perez. Theresa, Savannah is one of our best students and you would do well to spend a little time with her." Looking Theresa in her eyes, the teacher continued, "Maybe some of Savannah's ways will wipe off on you."

Then, Mrs. Wynn turned and walked out, leaving me and Theresa standing there. I had no idea what to do, but Theresa did. She folded her arms and looked me up and down.

"So, *Chica*...you're the good girl, huh?"

I didn't know how I was supposed to answer that, so I said nothing.

"Well, since I can't get kicked out of any more schools, and I don't like anybody else in this school, I might as well hang with you."

That didn't sound like a ringing endorsement for friendship, but she told me to walk with her back to Mrs. Wynn's classroom so that she could get her bag.

I agreed, but on the way, I just had to ask, "What happened? Why did she bring you to Mr. Bates' office?"

She shrugged. "That stupid boy called me out of my name so I punched him in his mouth. Not my fault that a couple of his teeth fell out. He won't do it again."

"Wow!" I didn't know if should be scared of her or impressed with her.

"Why you say wow?" She didn't let me answer. "That's how we do things where I come from. You want respect you have to demand it." She balled up her fist and twisted it around in her other hand.

From that point on, we were friends, best friends because Theresa told me that we would be. But it didn't take long for me to agree.

Theresa was everything that I wanted to be: feisty, outspoken, honest, direct...and all these years later, she still didn't take any mess.

I never did find out what that boy called her, but she made it clear that it wasn't her name. Not that it mattered to me. After hanging out with her for about three weeks, she was my girl. And now, after all these years, she was my sister.

"And anyway," Theresa broke through my memories, "I knew you didn't want no fried chicken and greens when you were home getting *steak*, if you know what I mean." She laughed again. "So why you on my phone? You finish with your steak already? That was *rapido*." This time she laughed so loud, I had to move the phone away from my ear. "Either y'all getting old or you need to learn some more tricks, *Mami*."

Why did Theresa have to go there? I had to learn new tricks? Is that why Sheldon had stepped out on me?

It was because of her last question that I just blurted it out. "Sheldon had a heart attack and he's here, at Howard. Can you come?"

"Oh, my goodness! Why didn't you say anything? Why didn't you stop me from talking? Oh, my goodness. Of course, I'll be there; I'm coming right now."

"Thank you."

"A heart attack," she continued. Through the phone, I heard plates clinging and pots clanging and I imagined that she'd been in her kitchen, whipping up her famous, elaborate brunch-for-one that she prepared every Saturday. "Oh, Vannie, you must be worried sick. What did the doctors say?"

"They've been in there with him for a few hours, but no one has told me anything. The nurse promised that someone would be out here soon."

"Well, that's all going to change when I get there," she said. "Hang tight. Everything will be all right. God is in control and you know God."

Yes, I knew God, but I didn't know anything about this—a cheating husband.

Normally, if I'd felt off-kilter about anything, Theresa would be my anchor. I took all of my questions and concerns to her. And in truth, my thrice-divorced Latina friend would have been the perfect person to help me figure out what was going on now. She would be able to track down Sheldon's mystery woman since she'd been an expert at finding each one of her ex-husbands' side chicks.

But I just couldn't bring myself to say a word. Theresa had so many years of 'I told you so's' built up inside of her just waiting for me. Even though Theresa loved me, loved Sheldon, and me and Sheldon together, this situation would prove her thesis that all men (no matter how lovable) were low-down, dirty dogs. Not that she would necessarily tell me to leave Sheldon's cheating behind. No, she was more likely to encourage me to figure out a way to stick it out until I couldn't take it anymore.

I could hear her now: "Sheldon was just doing what all men do, so why you gonna leave him because he's a natural liar and a cheat?"

Of course, Theresa had left each one of *her* husbands at the first sign of infidelity, but I had a feeling, she wouldn't want that for me—at least not right away.

Anyway, I couldn't wait for her to get here and after I reassured her that I would be fine until she arrived, we hung up.

I was so tempted to continue to snoop through Sheldon's emails, texts, and call log, but there was that call that I had to make to Kym.

I pressed the key for Kym's number and then wondered if she would even be home on a Saturday afternoon. Classes were over, she'd taken her last final last Friday. So, she was free to enjoy the holidays.

Except now, there wouldn't be so much joy. How in the world would I explain this to her? What words could I use to get her to understand, but keep her calm at the same time?

I had to come up with something because you see, Kym was...special. God may have selected me to be Sheldon's rib, but He made Kym Sheldon's heart.

Sometimes I wondered if my daughter remembered that she had a mother. I knew she loved me, at least she did deep down in the way that all children were supposed to love their parents.

But there was not a single doubt about how much she loved her father. To Kym, Sheldon was one step below Jesus. He could do no wrong, which meant I was never right.

I was never *that* offended since Kyle felt that way about me. Kyle was as much of a Mama's Boy as Kym was a Daddy's Girl.

This would've been so much easier if I were calling my son. But now that I had a couple of minutes to think about it, calling Kyle wouldn't do any good, at least not right now. While Kyle was a Journalism major at Hampton University, he'd been in Italy for the last three months working on a documentary about Americans who now made their home in that European country. He wouldn't be back to the States until the beginning of the year.

But Kym, who was a Biology major at Howard and studying to be a doctor, was right around the corner; so I had to call her.

The phone had barely rung once before she answered with an excited, "Daddddyyy. Are you home?"

"No sweetheart. It's not Daddy, it's just me."

"Oh, hello, Mother. Why are you calling from daddy's phone? Did you lose yours in your purse?" She laughed. She'd heard Sheldon say that joke to me many times and any other time I would have laughed with her.

But the back of my throat had grown dry and felt like it was swelling. Maybe my body was trying to protect me. Trying to make sure that I wouldn't be able to speak a word.

I had to do this, though. So, I inhaled, then exhaled knowing that there was no good way to be the bearer of bad news.

"Mother?" Kym called into the phone.

There was already distress in her voice, and I guess I'd taken too long to get my words together.

"Are you all right?" She didn't wait for me to answer. "Where's daddy? Is he there? Let me speak to him."

I needed to tell my child something. Taking a deep breath, I exhaled the words, "I'm...at...the...hospital."

"What happened?"

"I'm at Howard," I said, not answering her question.

I guess that was all right, because she said, "I'm on my way," with her voice trembling.

I was a little surprised that she didn't ask me again what happened, and I figured at this point, it would be better to tell her in person.

"I'll find you." Then my daughter hung up.

I prayed that it would be easier to tell her this news face-to-face. She'd be distraught once she found out. She'd need me to hold her, console her and assure her that her father would be well.

It was only going to take Kym minutes to get to me. And even Theresa—even though she was coming from downtown, that wasn't far away and she'd rent a jet if she thought that would get her to me faster.

So that meant that I didn't have much time to go through Sheldon's phone without having to explain my actions.

I went straight to the call log and searched. There were calls from me, to me, from the children, to the children, from his office, to his office. I scrolled and scrolled. Looking for that one number that I didn't recognize. I scrolled through what felt like hundreds of telephone numbers.

There was nothing.

I turned to the texts. Text after text.

And then....

Have you told Savannah? At least, tell Savannah.

My heart.

I read the text again, then searched for a response from Sheldon. But there didn't appear to be one.

My heart.

I read the text over and over, though I didn't need to read those eight words anymore. I knew them by heart.

My heart couldn't take it.

This was it.

And every part of me trembled.

"Mother!"

I felt like I jumped twelve feet out of my seat as the phone flew from my hand. I leaned forward, trying to catch it. But I failed; it crashed to the floor.

Before I could grab it, Kym did.

"Mother, what's going on?" she asked, handing the phone to me.

I wanted to answer my child, I really did. But that message. I had to read that message again. Because maybe I'd missed something. Maybe I'd skipped a word—or something.

Looking down at the phone, I pressed the home button. "Mother!"

Ugh! I wanted to scream. The screen...on the phone... was black! I pressed the home button again. And again. And again.

Still black.

I needed to see that message!

"Mother!" This time, Kym grabbed my shoulder. "What. Are. You. Doing. Here? Where is Daddy?"

When I looked up, she squatted so that even as I sat we were eye-to-eye.

My plan had been to prep her a little for the news. But I hadn't had time to think through that plan since I was so busy trying to figure out why my marriage was over. So the words leapt from my lips without any kind of filter, "Your father had a heart attack."

"What?" she screamed and jumped up. "Oh, my God, Mother. Is he going to be all right?"

I glanced around the waiting room, but even with the commotion that Kym and I were causing, not a soul seemed to notice. Or maybe it was that not a soul cared.

Reaching for my daughter's hand, I pulled her down into the seat next to me.

"I don't know, sweetheart. No one has told me anything yet."

Her butt had barely touched the seat and she was up again. "Well somebody better tell me something," she said, her voice filled with anger and attitude.

"Sweetheart," I said, working hard to keep my voice calmer than I felt. "We can't disturb the doctors. We have to let them do what they do so that they can save your father."

"Save him?" She pressed her hand over her mouth as if that could hold back her cries.

It didn't.

She trembled as I wrapped my arms around her. Or did the shaking come from me? I couldn't tell. But when I stepped back, the fear I saw in her eyes was exactly what I felt—except, my fear was fused with anger and heartache leaving me with a jumbled mess of emotions.

But at least I had enough in me to calm my daughter down. We sat down and when she leaned over and rested her head on my shoulder, I wrapped my arm around her shoulders. It felt so good to hold her this way and I was taken back to that time when she always needed me. Because no matter how much she loved her daddy, when she was sick, she wanted her mommy. And I was glad that I could be here for her now.

"Mommy, was he conscious when they brought him in?"

Mommy. Not Mother.

"Yes, sweetheart. And he must be responding now or else the doctors would not have been back there with him so long."

"That makes sense," she said more for herself than me.

Then, we sat. In silence. Well, in silence for the two of us. Above our heads, that TV that hung in the corner still played. But in our world...we were silent.

Until I heard Theresa. I heard my friend before I saw her.

It was all the Spanish that she spoke that let me know it was her. The Spanish, mixed with English, and her volume. So much volume for such a little person.

If Kym hadn't been here, I would've met her at the door, but I wasn't going to let go of my daughter. Theresa would find us.

And she did.

She walked into the room wearing a mink coat atop a black turtleneck and black jeans that were stuffed inside over-the-knee black suede boots.

My she-would-have-been-a-model-if-she-were-a-foot-taller friend had arrived.

"Vannie," she called out to me with her arms open wide, ready to embrace me. "Honey. I came as fast as I could and I prayed all the way over in the taxi."

I didn't take my arms away from my daughter, so Theresa leaned over and kissed me, before she kissed Kym, too.

When she sat on the other side of me, she asked, "So, what happened?"

"I don't know," I said.

"He was in the house with you when he got sick?" Theresa continued her questions. "Had he just gotten home? You know I want to know everything."

Both Kym and Theresa knew that Sheldon always took the red eye from Los Angeles to DC, not wanting to wait to the next day to travel. Because according to Sheldon, that would have been another day without me.

All this time, I had believed him. But now I was pretty sure his sacrificing a good night's sleep to get back to the East coast had nothing to do with me.

"Mommy, had Daddy just gotten home?" Kym repeated Theresa's question. "When he had the heart attack?"

"Yes. I mean, no. He hadn't been home long. He was home long enough to take a shower, and then he came out."

I stopped there, hoping that would be enough. But Kym and Theresa looked at me like they were waiting for the rest of the story.

The only thing was—I didn't know what I was supposed to say. There was no way I was going to tell them that I was pounding on his chest when he collapsed to the floor. They'd ask why, of course.

And then, there was the little thing about my daughter and her love for her father. Kym would scream that I had tried to murder Sheldon and I wasn't convinced that she wouldn't call the police.

So I only continued with, "He came out of the shower and we...talked a little bit before he fell and clutched his chest." That was kind of the truth.

"Oh, God!"

Kym sobbed and I held my daughter as my friend asked, "So that's it?"

I nodded because I didn't want to keep lying out loud.

"*Me estás tomando el pelo*. There was nothing else that caused it?" Theresa asked, acting like an interrogator. "I mean, what were you talking about when he collapsed? Was he upset?"

"He wasn't upset," I started, "but I don't think talking can cause a heart attack." I kinda snapped, giving Theresa a little attitude. But what else was I supposed to say? What was I supposed to do? I had to shut down the questions.

"Well, that's true," Theresa said doing something that she never did. "*Lo siento*." Then she backed down.

Kym laid her head on my shoulder again. "I'm just glad you were with him, Mommy. Can you imagine what it would have been like if you weren't there?"

If I wasn't there, none of this would have happened.

"I don't even want to think about it," Kym said. "Thank you, Mommy for being there for Daddy."

I held her a little tighter. "You're welcome, sweetheart. You're welcome."

And then I closed my eyes and prayed that my daughter never found out the truth.

Chapter
FOUR

"M rs. Hudson."

I glanced up. The doctor who'd met us at the ambulance stood in the waiting room door.

Kym, Theresa and I jumped up together, but I held up my forefinger, letting him know that I was the one that he wanted.

"I'm Mrs. Hudson."

He nodded a little, then glanced at Kym and then Theresa. He said, "May I speak with you...privately?"

I shook my head. "No, I mean, yes. But you can speak in front of them," I said, looking from side to side. "This is my daughter, and my...sister."

"Okay, follow me."

My heart felt like it was having its own attack as we walked behind the doctor. He led us into a room that was only large enough to hold a small table and a few chairs.

He motioned for us to sit down, but I was the only one who did. Kym stood on one side of me and Theresa was on the other.

For the first time, I got a good look at the doctor and I wondered why he was a doctor? He could have made a lot more money just playing one on TV because he surely looked more like an actor than someone with a medical degree.

The doctor sat across from me and held a tablet in his hand. "First of all, I don't think I had the opportunity to introduce myself to you. I'm Doctor Nichols, the Chief of Cardiology."

We all nodded, though we didn't say a word.

"Your husband did have a heart attack," he said so matter-of-factly that I had to ask him to repeat what he'd said.

Kym reached for my hand and I held her.

The doctor continued, "We've performed a series of tests and have discovered two blockages in your husband's arteries. And one blockage is so severe that it's only operating at ten percent of capacity."

Kym, Theresa and I gasped in unison. Not that I was sure that any of us understood the doctor's words—well, maybe Kym did. But I didn't.

I didn't have to understand, though. I could feel how serious this was.

"So, we need to perform surgery right away."

"When?" I asked, not understanding completely what 'right away' meant.

"In the next hour. This is an emergency and we want to prevent anymore life threatening issues."

Kym's grip on my hand tightened. "Life threatening?"

I could hear the tears and the fear in my daughter's voice.

She said, "Is my dad going to be all right?" Then, she begged, "Please tell me that he's going to be fine."

Before the doctor could answer, Theresa spoke. "Yes, Kymmie. Your daddy is going to be fine. God is in control and I know He won't let anything happen to your father."

Since Theresa was standing behind me, I couldn't see her face. But just the force of her voice let me know that my friend was sure of what she'd just said.

Now, it was the doctor's turn. "We'll do our best," he said.

"Thank you, Doctor," I said.

"I'm going to have the nurse bring in some forms that we'll need you to sign."

"Are you going to perform the surgery now?" Theresa asked.

The doctor nodded. "I won't be the one doing the surgery, but we do want to get him in there right away."

Kym asked. "Can we see him?"

"He's unconscious," the doctor explained.

"Yes, but I have to see him," Kym said as if her next breath depended on it.

The doctor paused just for a few seconds. "Of course. We're going to prep him, but then you'll be able to see him. But just for a few moments."

Then, Dr. Nichols looked at me as if he expected me to have questions. But I didn't. My heart was so split. I didn't know what to feel, so I certainly didn't know what to say.

Dr. Nichols said, "You can stay in this room, and one of the nurses will be right in."

The next minutes were a fusion of moving at the speed of light, but then feeling like time had just about stopped. The nurse brought me the forms, Theresa read them, I signed them, and Kym cried.

Then the nurse said, "Give us a few minutes and we'll take you to see your husband."

While we waited, we sat in the waiting room, quiet, each caught up in our own thoughts, asking our own questions, praying for our own answers.

Then, "Oh, my God, Mother, we have to call Kyle."

I nodded. "But I don't know if we should call him now. I mean, there's nothing he can do so far away."

"He'll want to know, he'll want to come home."

I didn't know if that was the right thing.

But then, Theresa said, "Kymmie's right. You have to call Kyle."

They were right. I knew that. So, I pulled Sheldon's phone from purse, but again, when I hit the Home button, the screen stayed black.

"Daddy's phone is dead, Mother. Use mine."

Kyle answered after just a couple of rings, but he didn't exactly say hello.

"Can't talk now, Kymmie. I'm on this hot date with this Italian chick and...."

"Kyle, it's me," I said, not wanting to hear his next words about him and some Italian chick.

"Mom! What's wrong? Why are you calling from Kym's phone?"

"I'm at the hospital, son." And then, I went on to tell him the story I'd told Kym and Theresa and added the part about his father's surgery.

"I'll catch the first flight, Mom."

"Kyle, I'm not sure...why don't you wait until we know something."

"I already know enough, Mom. I know that I need to be there with you and Dad."

"You know your father would want you to finish out your project."

"I know, but this changes everything."

"Why don't you do me a favor, Kyle? Let's wait until after the surgery."

"I don't know...."

"You wouldn't be able to get here in time anyway; they're going to take him in a few minutes. So even if you caught the next flight...."

"Okay, but will you promise to call me?"

"Of course I will."

"And Mom, I'm praying. Dad's gonna be all right, okay?"

"Okay," I said, wanting to weep.

"I love you, Mom. I love you so much."

And then, I couldn't help it; a few tears slipped from my eyes.

He hung up, and I almost wanted to call him right back. Tell him to come now because I needed him. I needed everyone I loved to be around me.

But all I did was hand the phone to Kym right before the nurse came into the room.

"I'm going to take you to your husband." She paused. "Really, you're supposed to go in one at a time."

All three of us were shaking our heads before she even got her words all the way out. She could try, but that wasn't going to happen. I needed Kym and Kym needed me and we both needed Theresa. That was the only way that it was going to work.

We followed the nurse through the long hallway to the room at the end of the hall. Dr. Nichols was standing outside as we approached.

He turned to us and said, "Mrs. Hudson, I'm glad you're here. I want you to meet Dr. Bartholomew. He's the lead cardiologist on your husband's case."

The white-haired doctor gave me a toothy grin, but I couldn't stop staring at the way he was bent over slightly. And was that a hump in his back?

"You're the lead cardiologist?" Kym asked, her shock was all in her voice and on her face.

I held my breath, waiting for my daughter to ask the question that I knew was on all of our minds—just how old was this man? I didn't have a number, couldn't take a guess. But the word elderly described him best. Wasn't there a retirement age for doctors?

Dr. Bartholomew nodded. "I'll be taking care of your father."

Dr. Nichols made all of the introductions, then said, "I'm going to leave you with Doctor Bartholomew. You can trust that you're in good hands."

As he turned to walk away, Theresa stopped him. "Why can't you perform the surgery?"

I'd been thinking Kym was the one I had to watch. I should've known the real one was the feisty one.

The way the doctor turned around, then gave Theresa a long glance up, then a long glance down, then smiled, let me know that the doctor thought my friend was flirting, or maybe he hoped that she was.

If this were any other time, any other place, I would've told the doctor the truth—that he needed to sniff around somewhere else because when Theresa looked at him, she didn't see the brown-eyed Adonis that the rest of the world gave him credit for being. She saw a two-legged canine who would bite her and give her rabies the first chance he had.

"I promise that you are in the best hands." He smiled, pivoted, and kept on moving.

"The best old hands," Kym muttered, just loud enough for me to hear.

I prayed that the doctor hadn't heard my daughter and didn't see the doubt in my friend's eyes. If this was the man who was going to take care of my husband, we didn't need to insult him.

But really, my daughter and friend were just saying what I thought. Was this doctor even aware of new medical technology? Would his age hinder him from giving Sheldon the best care? Could he even see?

While the questions swirled in my mind, Dr. Bartholomew explained his plans for Sheldon's surgery and what we should expect afterward.

"He's unconscious right now, but Doctor Nichols said that you wanted to see him."

"Yes," Kym said in a nicer, calmer tone. "Just for a couple of minutes.

"That will be fine, but the nurse will ask you to leave in a few minutes. We want to get him into surgery right away."

Then, he pushed the door to the room open and I walked in first with Kym and Theresa so close behind me. My eyes were on the center of the room. The bed where Sheldon laid. I wondered if I'd be able to get close to him; I wasn't sure because of all the machines that surrounded him. Machines with their green squiggly lines and three-second interval beeps.

But I was able to get close, up to the rail. And I looked down at my husband. He was so still, and the blessing was that he looked like he was thinking.

Thank God, because I was afraid that he might already look like he was dead.

"Daddy."

Just that quickly, I'd forgotten that Kym and Theresa were with me. I kept my eyes on Sheldon while I reached, then grasped Kym's hand.

"Daddy," she called out again. "Please. Please don't die." With her free hand, she reached for his. And as she held his hand, she squeezed mine tighter.

"Please, Daddy," she cried. "Mommy and I need you. And Kyle does, too. Please don't die."

Behind me, Theresa sniffled, but still, she whispered in Kym's ear, "He's not going to die. The doctors will make sure of that because God will guide them. All you have to do is tell your daddy that you love him. And that you'll see him in a little while."

A tear fell from Kym's eye to my hand.

Theresa encouraged, "Go on, Kymmie. Tell your daddy that you're waiting for him to wake up and then, we should give your mom a little time alone with him."

I wasn't expecting that; I wasn't even sure that I wanted to be alone with Sheldon. The last time we were alone, it hadn't worked out too well for him.

Kym leaned over the bed's rail and kissed Sheldon's cheek. "I love you, Daddy," she cried, then released me before she rushed out of the room.

Theresa stayed behind for a moment longer, resting her hand on Sheldon's chest. She closed her eyes and muttered what I thought was a prayer. But her voice was low, and she spoke in Spanish, so I didn't know exactly what she was saying.

I was thankful, though. Theresa had no faith in men; every bit of faith she had was in God...and I guess that was the way it was supposed to be.

When she opened her eyes, she squeezed my shoulder. "You stay a little while, Vannie." When the nurse glanced at us, Theresa told her, "This is her husband. It will just be for a little while."

The nurse raised her eyebrows, but said nothing and then, Theresa stepped out of the room.

I moved closer to the bed and grasped the handrails. In retrospect, it was good that I was alone with Sheldon right now. Because if Kym and Theresa were in here, they would wonder why I wasn't touching Sheldon, or trying to hold him, or kiss him.

Really, I wanted to do all of that. I wanted to beg him to come back to me so that I could love him again.

But then my cracked heart asked why did I want him to come back when it was clear that he didn't love me?

So, I said nothing. And just stared. And watched his chest rise and fall, rise and fall.

Inside my head, I asked him all the questions that I needed to ask, but aloud, I only said, "Why, Sheldon?"

"Oh, Mrs. Hudson, I'm sure your husband didn't want this to happen," the nurse said, clearly having no idea what my question meant. "We're going to work very hard to get him back to you."

I nodded.

The door to the hospital room opened and a team of nurses entered. The nurse who'd been with me, said, "I'm sorry, Mrs. Hudson."

I held up my hand, signaling that I knew it was time. Taking a final look at my husband, I leaned forward to kiss him, but halfway to his lips, I stopped. All I could muster was, "Sheldon, I need you, we all need you to make it."

And then, I walked past all the nurses, the team that would be working to keep Sheldon alive. I stepped outside of his room and stopped. Leaning against the wall, I closed my eyes and all I could get out was, "Please, God." But I was pretty sure that was enough.

With a sigh, I opened my eyes.

And stared right into the eyes of Ginger.

Chapter
FIVE

I came as fast as I could, how's Sheldon?" Ginger asked as she wrapped me inside her arms.

I said nothing, not even when she stepped back and stared into my eyes, frowning as if she was trying to figure out what was wrong with me, why I was mute?

It was just that I couldn't say anything. Not as I stood there, staring at her draped in a red turtleneck and black skinny jeans that celebrated every curve on her size four frame. Not to mention her blonde weave that was an expensive imitation of Beyoncé's style. Even her leather hobo purse was a fashion statement.

Then, there were her stilettos. Even in this weather, with snow on the ground and more on the way, she wore pencil-thin heels that were at least four-inches high.

And they were red!

It was her!

But it couldn't be.

Not Ginger Clark, Sheldon's long-time right-hand assistant whom I'd always liked. She'd started with him when she graduated from college with a degree in Business Administration. She'd been the perfect fit to Sheldon's electronic company and into our family, coming to all kinds of holiday dinners and family celebrations.

No, it couldn't be her.

But then...how did Ginger know that Sheldon was in the hospital? Sheldon hadn't called nor texted her to tell her that he was back; not only had he not had time, but I'd searched all the messages.

Maybe she had changed her number. Maybe she had a number that only Sheldon knew. Maybe she was the sender of that mystery text.

"Savannah," she called my name as if she were concerned, "are you all right?"

Before I could answer, Kym rushed toward us.

"Ginger, thank you for coming!" Kym held the woman that she'd known since she was thirteen. "Daddy would want you here with us. You're like family."

"I wouldn't want to be anywhere else." Turning back to me, she said, "Are you okay, Savannah?"

I nodded.

Ginger asked, "Can I get you water or anything?"

I shook my head.

I guess my daughter realized that I couldn't use my words right now, so she jumped in. "It's just been a lot on us, you know." Kym held my hand as if I were the child and she led me to the waiting room.

Ginger walked with us. She said, "I would have been here sooner, but my plane just landed. When I turned on the phone and got your message, I headed straight over here."

"You just landed?" I stopped moving. "From where?"

She waved her hand. "Oh, I was just away," she said and glanced down as if she didn't want to look into my eyes.

Oh. My. God. She'd been away with Sheldon and she had just let that slip. Of course, they wouldn't fly back on the same flight; they couldn't take the chance since I'd been known to surprise Sheldon at the airport a few times. But they hadn't been careful enough because I had just found out.

Kym was oblivious to my discovery, and she kept on talking to the enemy. "They're getting Daddy prepped for surgery," she explained.

"Oh, no. It's that bad?" Ginger asked.

"The doctors told us that surgery is a good thing. It's going to save his life."

Kym took over the duties of explaining what was going on as we stepped back into the waiting room. I sat down next to Theresa, who stood to hug Ginger. And as she did that, I sat back. And studied this tart, this traitor.

I tried to recall every time I'd seen Sheldon and Ginger together. Had they ever done anything inappropriate in front of me? Had they snuck kisses behind my back? Or worse, had they had a five-minute sexual rendezvous one Thanksgiving, in our home, in one of the bedrooms while everyone else was downstairs?

My blood pressure was rising, rising, rising. How had I ever called this woman a friend? How had I not seen what she was doing with my husband?

I'd been bamboozled and it was my fault. How often had I heard that women should never trust women? And with a name like Ginger, why hadn't I been concerned? I had never considered it before, but there were only two reasons why anyone would have that name: 1—you're a stripper. 2—you're a husband stealer.

"You know those shoes are fierce," Kym said to Ginger when they finally all sat down and my eyes went straight to those shoes that matched the thong. My daughter continued, "I have no idea how you can walk in them."

"Especially in the snow," Theresa added.

"These are my favorite." Ginger stretched out her leg as if she wanted to make sure that we all got a good look. "I hardly take them off."

The three of them chuckled, but I didn't do anything but stare, thinking that if she didn't pull her leg back soon, I was going to break it.

I could imagine those legs in those shoes, strutting around some Los Angeles hotel room as she put on a show for Sheldon. Wearing nothing but that thong and those stilettos.

"I know Daddy loved it."

Kym's words made me jerk my head back. Sheldon loved what?

Then, I tuned in to their conversation that had turned to Bubba burgers.

"That's where we had lunch on Monday before we both went to the airport to catch our flights."

She'd slipped again. Giving me more and more information. By the time Sheldon came out of surgery, I might have a confession.

Maybe she would tell me everything: how Sheldon drooled over her when she stepped out of the shower. How she purred as she passed by him so that he could appreciate all that she had to offer. How she had kissed him with such passion and they'd had sex for hours and hours and hours.

The thought of that just made me mad. Sheldon didn't have to turn to Ginger for sex. Yes, we'd been married for twenty-three years, but Sheldon and I did pretty well together. That was the best kind of sex, when you knew your partner so well. And we had sex often enough; Sheldon certainly wasn't starving.

So why had he turned to her?

"Mother? Mother!"

I blinked myself back to the waiting room. "Yes," I said, focusing on Kym.

"Theresa and I are going down to the cafeteria. What do you want us to bring you?"

"Nothing."

"Mother, you have to eat."

"She's right, Vannie. So what you want?"

Before Ginger could add her two cents that I would throw back in her face, I said, "Just bring me a sandwich. Any sandwich."

"We'll be right back, Mother," Kym said as she planted a kiss on my cheek.

"Don't worry, I'll stay here with her." There was Ginger's two cents.

And just like I promised, I gave it back to her. "No, you go on with them."

"You shouldn't be alone," Theresa told me. Then, to Ginger, she said, "You stay here with her."

If they kept pushing it, I was going to stand up and yell and tell everyone in this hospital what this skank had done. So before I caused that kind of scene, I said, "The three of you, go to the cafeteria. I'm going to the chapel and I'm going to do that by myself!"

Not waiting for anyone's approval or thoughts, I stomped out of the room with extra heavy steps so that no one would even consider coming after me. I had no idea where I was going, no idea what floor the chapel was on, but I'd find it.

I needed to go there anyway. By myself. Because there were a few things that I wanted to say to God and a few things that He needed to explain to me.

Chapter
SIX

I sat on the front row of the first floor chapel, staring at the golden cross that hung high in the middle of the wall in front of me.

I hadn't been sure of what to expect when I walked in here; I figured this was a hospital, this was the weekend, so every seat in the chapel would be filled with family and friends of patients praying their loved ones back to good health.

But when I pulled open the huge mahogany door and peeked inside, I was shocked to see the empty space. No one was in there at all...well, except for maybe God. So, I had rushed inside and taken this seat.

Now that I sat here, though, I wasn't sure what to do. Should I go up to the kneeling bench and pray? That didn't seem like the appropriate place for me to be with some of the questions I had for God.

In the end, though, all I asked Him was, "Why?"

And God answered me, the way He always did. But His answer didn't make any sense.

No.

So, I repeated the question to God: *Why did Sheldon cheat on me?*

No.

I was sitting in a chapel, but clearly God wasn't hearing me because His answer didn't match up with my question.

No.

I just sat there, for about an hour. Asking the same question, over and over. But I didn't get an answer—I just kept hearing *No*.

So, I stopped asking; just sat and stared at the cross. And then, God brought something to my memory. The first time, that Sheldon and I seriously talked about a future together....

"What's your last name?" Sheldon asked as he placed a small plastic spoon full of ice cream into my mouth.

"You know my last name," I said through the black cherry delight that melted on my tongue.

"But, I want to hear you say it." And then, he fed me another spoonful.

This time, I savored the flavor of the ice cream until it vanished. Then, I said, "How am I suppose to answer you if you keep feeding me ice cream?"

"Just answer the question." He tapped my lips playfully with the spoon.

"Hudson. My last name is Hudson. I'm Savannah Hudson."

He leaned back in the plastic chair outside of the ice cream shoppe where we'd stopped to enjoy dessert after our movie date. "Ahhh. I love it when you say that." Then, he gave me a quick peck on the lips. "I keep telling you that's a sign. You're supposed to marry me because you won't even have to change your last name."

It had been funny to me when we first met at a job fair that was held at the DC Convention Center. We'd both stopped at the same time in front of Apple, the hot new tech company.

The recruiter standing there told us that he'd just talk to us at the same time. I'd introduced myself first as Savannah Hudson. A second later, he'd introduced himself as Sheldon Hudson.

The recruiter had looked from one to the other and then asked, "Are you brother and sister?"

"Oh, no!" I said, though I did smile, thinking that was funny. Sheldon laughed. "No, she's not my sister. She's my wife."

Now, that I didn't find funny. Especially when the recruiter believed him.

But Sheldon had followed me down each aisle that day until I finally gave him my number. He'd called that night, and the next, and the next. Until I finally invited him to visit me in my Georgetown University apartment.

That had been three months ago and I guess we were a couple now. Especially since Sheldon really loved to talk about marriage. More than any guy (or girl for that matter) that I had ever met.

"There are just too many signs that God lined up for us. Your last name is the same as mine to make it easy."

"Hmmmm," was all I said.

"We were born on the same day, so we'll never get into a fight because I forgot your birthday."

That was true.

"And we were born the same year, so I'll never forget how old you are."

Whenever he talked about all the coincidences of the two of us, I had to admit, it was so strange.

But not strange to Sheldon.

He said, "We were destined to be together from birth. That's what God's telling us." Then, his face became long and serious, and his eyes darkened a little. Something that I had noticed happened when Sheldon was in deep thought.

"I mean it Savannah, I want to marry you."

I leaned away from him. "Married? Don't you think it's a little soon to talk about marriage?"

"No, not when we've been given all these signs. And come on, we've known each other for three months already."

His words were crazy, but his tone made it sound so logical.

"We can't get married. We're too young. What about finishing college? And then, what about life after college? We have the whole world to see."

"Maybe you do, but I am looking at my world."

Like the ice cream I'd just eaten, I melted. And my heart swelled with a feeling that I'd never felt before. I'd been in a couple of relationships, here and there during the three years I'd been at Georgetown. But none of them felt real to me. None of them felt like this.

Not that I was looking. My parents had an education fund for me from the time I was born, knowing that I would go to college. Even after they passed away in a car accident when I was twelve, my grandmother picked up their pledge that I would be well-educated. I was at Georgetown to get a degree other than MRS.

And I wasn't even thinking about marriage after graduation. I had other plans for a Bachelor's in Technology Management: I was going to work for one of the country's top tech companies for a few years before I started my own, then, I'd become the first black female tech entrepreneur, famous for inventing a computer watch, something that had fascinated me since I was a child and watched The Jetsons.

But Sheldon was beginning to have me reassess my life in the light of love.

Right before we left the ice cream shoppe, he said,

"I promise to love you and only you for the rest of my life, Savannah Hudson."

"Really, Sheldon Hudson?"

He raised his right hand and placed the left one over his heart. "I swear on everything."

Sitting here now, in this chapel, I could almost hear those words. As if he'd just spoken them into my ear.

I had been so sure that he was telling me the truth. It was in the way he'd spoken those words, the solemness of his tone, that made me believe him.

Almost two years to the day of that April conversation, one year after I received my degree from Georgetown and he received his from Howard, we were united as husband and wife.

From the day we exchanged our vows, I never had any doubts that Sheldon would love, honor, and cherish me every day that he was alive....

It wasn't until I raised my eyes, glancing once again at the cross that I felt the tears roll down my cheeks.

There was so much inside each tear I shed. I was scared; scared that I could lose Sheldon. That his heart attack could take him away from all of us.

And then, I was scared; scared that his heart had already been taken from me.

So, I just sat in that chapel and cried. Cried for a love that I could lose, and cried for a love that I was afraid had already been lost.

Chapter SEVEN

I stayed in the chapel as long as I could before I was sure Kym or Theresa would come looking for me. Or worse— they could have sent Ginger and that would've been a whole 'nother story. A fight in a hospital chapel that would have been worthy of being on the front page of the National Enquirer.

So, I'd returned (reluctantly) to the waiting room where Theresa said, "I was just about to send out the calvary for you, Vannie."

I told her that I knew that, I told Kym that I was fine, and I ignored Ginger. Taking the sandwich from my daughter, I nibbled as we waited, and waited and waited.

The hours passed so slowly, the day faded to night. And time ticked by...from five to six, six to seven, seven to eight.

Kym, Theresa, Ginger and I paced. And they talked. (I only talked when spoken to.) And we watched mindless television.

But mostly we paced. And prayed. All of us, even Ginger.

Sheldon's surgery had to be going well. The bad news would have been if the doctors had walked in here way before the five to six hours Dr. Bartholomew told us it would take. That would have been the tragedy if they'd come back and told us that there was nothing they could do to save him.

This was far better.

At least, that's what I kept telling myself.

A little after eight, Kym said, "Something must be wrong. They said they'd be done by now."

"I don't think so," Theresa and I said together. We looked at each other before I let Theresa continue.

"If something were wrong, the doctors would have been back sooner, not later," she said what I'd been thinking. "Your dad is fine. I told you that. *Dios todavía está en control.* Trust him."

Kym nodded, needing to believe that.

So we paced and prayed some more.

And then, right before the clock struck nine, Dr. Bartholomew appeared at the door. Still wearing his surgical trousers and shirt, with the mask hanging from his neck.

He smiled and looked just like an angel to me.

"It's done; it went well. Your husband made it through."

We stood and hugged each other. When Ginger turned to me, I faced the doctor. "So, what happens now?"

Kym stood by my side and held my hand as the doctor explained the next steps.

"Like I said, he's going to be in ICU for a couple of days. And that means that he's not out of the woods yet. But we're confident. Though tonight, we don't want him to have many visitors. He's unconscious, but he needs to rest."

We nodded our understanding and Kym cried when she said to the doctor, "Thank you." I think she shocked him a little when she pulled him into an embrace. "Thank you for saving my daddy."

Or maybe he wasn't shocked. Because the doctor hugged her back, told her she was welcome and it was his pleasure.

"Working on the heart is my passion," he said. "Now, he's going to be asleep for the rest of the night, so I would advise that you all go home and get some rest. He's going to need you well."

I was already shaking my head. There was no way I was going to leave Sheldon here alone. At least not on the first night. Even with all that I'd been feeling, what I felt most was that I was his wife—at least for now.

"I'm staying," I told the doctor, and then, I turned to Kym, Theresa, and Ginger, though I only made eye contact with my daughter and my friend.

"I need you to go home," I told them.

"I'm not leaving you here by yourself, Mother."

"I'll be here with her," Theresa said.

"No, you're going home, too."

They talked over each other, even Ginger, giving me all the reasons why each one of them should stay.

But I held up my hand. "I need all of you to go home and get some rest so that I can go home in the morning."

That quieted them down.

I continued, "We'll set this up in shifts so that someone is always here with Sheldon."

"Well...," Kym began though I heard her doubts.

"That makes sense, *Chica*," Theresa said and Ginger nodded.

"Okay, Mother, but I'm not happy about this."

"I know, but you're not that far away and if I need you, I promise I'll call."

I gave them all hugs, and this time, I even embraced Ginger. I had to since I didn't want to draw attention to the fact that I hated her. At least not yet.

We said goodbye at Sheldon's door, and when the three walked toward the elevator, I entered Sheldon's room. I paused for a moment at the door, taking in my husband. He really didn't look all that different than he did before—except for the big tube coming out of his mouth. It was attached to a machine and every few seconds a 'woosh' filled the room.

I moved from the door to the edge of his bed. There was such a potpourri of emotions stirring inside of me. No one in the world had ever gone through something like this—at least, I hoped not. I wouldn't want to wish this on anyone—this combination of love and hate, this contradiction of hope that someone lived and died. It was lethal to the heart.

Staring at his chest, I became hypnotized by the motion; the slow rise and fall. I wondered, what was it like for Sheldon? Did he have any idea of what was going on? Was he aware in any way or asleep and just dreaming? And if he were dreaming, was his mind filled with images of me or did I share his mental stage with Ginger? Or was I on his mind at all?

That thought made the other side of my heart click in and my fingers rolled around the rail. And I imagined that the rail was Sheldon's neck.

But then—hadn't I just prayed for him to be all right?

So, I changed my thought processes and imagined that this was Ginger's neck. Yes, that was better. That tiny, delicate neck—I could almost feel it beneath my fingers. Squeezing the breath, the life out of her.

But that only lasted for a few moments. Because hatred was exhausting. Or maybe it was just the emotions of this whole day that made me just so tired.

It hadn't even been a full day; that was hard to believe. Just about fifteen, sixteen hours since Sheldon had first come home.

And now, here we were.

"Your husband is resting comfortably," one of the nurses said. I turned around. "I'm going to leave this here for you." She placed a gray blanket on the two-cushioned sofa that I hadn't even noticed against the far wall.

"I can stay in here?"

The nurse nodded. "The doctors don't like that sometimes, but us nurses...we get it."

I thanked her and stayed by Sheldon's side until she left the room. Then, I sank into the softness of the sofa. Well, soft was an exaggeration; this wasn't nearly as comfortable as any of my furniture at home. But compared to the hard chairs in the waiting room, this felt like heaven.

I tucked my feet below me and positioned myself so that if Sheldon woke up and turned to his right, the first face he would see would be mine.

Then, if he'd been dreaming about Ginger, how would he feel?

It wasn't my plan to fall asleep, but exhaustion pulled me into unconsciousness, and took me to another Sheldon moment....

"Sheldon, where are we going? You've been driving for days."

He laughed. "It's only been ninety minutes. And anyway, do you have somewhere else to be, Mrs. Hudson?"

"Well no...."

Early this morning, Sheldon had awakened me and for a moment, I'd forgotten that it was Saturday. He'd had a few simple words: "Get up, we're going somewhere, it's a surprise, and don't ask any questions."

This wasn't the first time that Sheldon had done this. In the two years of our marriage, he was always up to something, surprising me in so many ways. And I loved it all.

But it didn't usually take this long. Most of the time we would just jump on the metro and we'd go to some new restaurant. Or we'd drive somewhere and stay a few nights in a swanky hotel.

This time, with the way Sheldon was leaned back and still driving down I-95, it didn't seem like a stop was anywhere in my near future.

"I really just want to know how much longer," I said.

"Why?"

"Because I'm hungry."

"Okay, so if I feed you, will you then sit back and enjoy the ride?"

"Feed me first," I pouted. "'Cause I'm not making any deals on an empty stomach."

He laughed, eased off the Interstate and pulled up to a drive-thru. "Order anything you want," he said. "Nothing is too good or too much for my wife."

I laughed as I took in the burger menu that didn't have a single item over four dollars.

"Laugh all you want," my husband said. "I've already gotten my first promotion, and the next one is on its way."

Sheldon was right about that. He was moving up fast at in the electronics division of Sony's DC office, which is where he'd been working since we graduated. I had no doubt that one day Sheldon would own that company.

After a couple of cheeseburgers, I was happy enough to lean back and do what Sheldon wanted me to do—I enjoyed the ride.

It was another hour and a half before, Sheldon pulled off the freeway and then another half an hour before he turned off the major road and drove deep into the woods.

"Where are we going?"

"Someplace where I will fulfill your every fantasy."

I didn't have very many of those, and I knew asking Sheldon to be more specific wouldn't get me far. Based on how long we'd been driving, I knew we were still in Virginia, the southern most part. I guess that was all Sheldon was going to give me.

Finally, he stopped the car in front of a huge log cabin, and I got my first clue.

"Wait right here," he said as he jumped out of the car.

I didn't do as I was told. I opened my door, stepped out of the car, then did a slow three-hundred-sixty degree spin taking in the beauty surrounding me. Of course I knew that God created the whole earth, but there were certain places where his creation seemed to be magnified. And this place was one of those. Trees that were so tall that their branches brushed the sky with leaves that celebrated the artistry of Autumn. There was no green anywhere. Just red, yellow, purple, orange, pink...blue! I'd never seen blue leaves before. But here they were. Leaves that were as blue as the sky that could not been seen through the thickness of the foliage.

Sheldon rushed out of the building jiggling keys. But he said nothing when he motioned for me to get back into the car.

The car wobbled over the uneven road, but just about a mile away, Sheldon stopped in front of a single cabin. "You go on inside," he said. "I'll grab our bags."

I stepped up the two wooden stairs and twisted the knob on the door. It opened and I entered into what I could only call a garden brought inside.

The same colors that were outside were inside the cabin: there were some plants that reached high to the ceiling with others that were just lush and wide.

The sofa table held a wide bowl filled with apples, and on what was the dining room table was another fruit centerpiece with pineapples, cherries, mangos and grapes.

The only thing that seemed to be out of place in this indoor Garden of Eden were the two wine stands on either side of the sofa, each with a bottle of wine.

I was still doing my self-tour when Sheldon busted through the door. "What do you think?" He dropped our bags on the floor.

"This is beautiful." I asked, "What kind of place is this?"

"I told you, this is a place where all of your fantasies can come true." He pulled me into his arms. "But if you must know, it's called Eve's Paradise."

I frowned.

"It's just a little retreat for lovers. And we are certainly lovers," he told me before he covered my lips with his and gave me one of those kisses that always led to something more.

With our lips still together, he backed me into the bedroom, then slipped my sweater from my shoulders, and unbuttoned my blouse. Sheldon was as skillful as a surgeon when it came to undressing me piece by piece, yet he kept our lips locked together.

By the time I was naked, I was ready for everything. But then, he pulled away and reached for something on the bed. I hadn't noticed it—some kind of outfit, a bathing suit, maybe.

"Put this on." He sounded like he was out of breath already.

That's why I didn't get it. I was naked and my husband wanted me to put on clothes?

I took a closer look as he said, "We're going to be Adam and Eve this weekend."

I examined the clothes, or rather lack of clothes that he wanted me to put on. "There's not much here," I said.

"Please."

It was only because Sheldon had probably spent a fortune on his fantasy. And then, there was the way he said please. How could any wife resist a husband who begged?

But then, I put it on.

What in the world? It was nothing but a thong bikini made out of fake leaves and flowers. The top was okay; I mean, everything was covered—barely.

But that piece that they called a bottom?

I was so glad that Sheldon pulled it off of me just as quickly as I'd put it on. Even for the two minutes that I'd worn it, twirling around so that Sheldon could enjoy every angle, it was the most uncomfortable thing I'd ever worn. That little strip that was called a thong served no purpose.

I'd rather be naked. In this case, bare was better....

As I came out of that memory, I thought about the fact that I'd never come close to wearing a thong again. So, was that what Sheldon was looking for? A woman who would wear a thong for him?

What was the big deal about a thong? I mean, it was so uncomfortable that I didn't wear it again for the rest of that weekend. Sheldon and I had just traipsed through the cabin naked for forty-eight hours. Wasn't that wonderful for a man?

In the years after, Sheldon had never asked me to wear anything like that again. Not that I would have done it, but was that what this was about? A pair of panties? Did Ginger fulfill fantasies for Sheldon that he knew he couldn't ask me?

As I had that thought, a cool breeze passed through the room, and I tightened the blanket around me. But as I tried to pull it closer, it slipped to the floor.

"Just great," I whispered, annoyed that I had to even open my eyes. I reached down, gathered the blanket, and then looked up...and into the most beautiful pair of brown eyes that I'd ever seen.

And then, I took in the whole face that the brown eyes belonged to.

Dang! For a moment, I thought I was awake. But this had to be one of those dreams where you thought you were awake, but you weren't.

I had no idea why my dream had taken such a sharp left turn, but I was sure glad that I ended up here.

And then, the vision of my dream spoke. "Hi," he said with a smile that was even more perfect than the strong line of his jaw, the squareness of his chin, and the two dimples that were carved deep into his cheeks.

"I'm Dr. David, your husband's heart specialist. I was just checking in on your husband."

Wait...what? Was I awake?

Mesmerized by those eyes, I sat all the way up. "You didn't wake me," I lied. And then, I put my hand to my mouth to do a quick breath check. I was good.

"What happened to Dr. Bartholomew?" I asked, though I honestly didn't care. This man was treating my husband? Shoot. Dr. Bartholomew could rest in peace. Not that I wanted him dead or anything. I just hoped that wherever he was, he was resting and would stay there for a long time.

And now I hoped Sheldon took his time waking up and getting well. After what he put me through, he owed me that.

"How did you sleep?" he asked.

"Okay, I guess. I don't think I've been asleep that long."
I rubbed my hands along my arms trying to warm myself. "I
just felt a little cold...suddenly."

"Well, I can fix that," he said in a voice that definitely fit
this man. One of those deep, baritone voices that was made
for singing, or preaching, or whispering sweet everythings
into a woman's ear.

"I'm going to get a cot for you and I'll bring you a few
more blankets. Do you need anything else?"

It sounded like Dr. David was about to make an exit.
And I wanted, I needed him to stay. For just a little longer.
With one hand, I smoothed out my hair and with the other,
I wiped the wrinkles out of my sweat pants.

Ugh! Sweat pants! Why did I have to be wearing sweats
the first time that this man saw me?

"No, I'm good," I finally told him. Then, as he picked up
the chart that was hooked to the edge of Sheldon's bed, I
asked again, "Where's Doctor Bartholomew?"

It was as if he didn't hear me. Because all he did was read,
then nod as if he agreed with what he was reading.

And he began humming. With the same baritone that
was in his voice. And in my head, I sang along....

I believe that we will be...in love eternally....

I couldn't believe he was humming my and Sheldon's
song!

I stared at him so hard, I was surprised that I couldn't see straight into his soul. This man was walking perfection, down to his fingertips. Every time he flipped a page on the chart, it looked like he was playing an instrument.

This had to be a dream.

That's why I closed my eyes again. Squeezed them tight for a couple of seconds to get that dream out of my mind.

So why did the humming stay?

"You will always be the one...for me...."

I opened my eyes, and he was right there. In front of me with his perfect brown eyes on mine.

I sighed.

He smiled.

Then, he moved toward the door. "I'll be right back."

The moment the door swung closed behind him, I jumped up, wishing I'd had the foresight to bring a change of clothes with me. Why hadn't I thought about the chances of running into a fine doctor? I was at Howard University Hospital, for goodness sakes!

Well, at least I could make sure my face looked good. I searched the room for a mirror. There was nothing. But I was resourceful if I wasn't anything else. So I used the single framed picture that was in the room. Of a little boy and a girl, holding hands by a pond.

That picture made me pause. Made me think about Kym and Kyle. Made me turn around and look at Sheldon.

My husband.

And of course that was the moment that Dr. David returned. Rolling a folded up cot with a couple of blankets over it.

He pushed the cot in front of the couch. "I'll get this set up for you," he said. He piled the stack of three blankets at the bottom of the cot, but I no longer needed them because I wasn't anywhere near cold.

As he spread out the sheet, I said, "I can do that."

"You don't think I can take care of these kinds of things? Because I'm a doctor?"

He laughed, and I laughed with him, but that wasn't what I was thinking at all. All I was thinking was that either he or I needed to go to the other side of the room because I needed a little bit of distance between us.

"No, I'm sure that you can make a bed," I said. "I was just thinking that I can do this myself."

"I know you can, but I'm here to help."

When he smoothed the sheet on top of the cot, he leaned so close that I couldn't help but take in the fragrance of his cologne. It was something that I'd never smelled before. A blend of ...everything: citrus and thyme, oak and musk. And there was even some...leather? Yes, leather.

I took two steps back from this man.

"How's that?" he said when he finished.

"Perfect." And I wasn't talking about the cot.

"Are you ready to climb in?" he asked.

Only if you climb in with me.

And then, I blushed. I mean, really blushed. Like blushed from the top of my head, all the way down to my five-year-old sneakers. I did one of those complete body blushes.

Because I had never in my life had a lustful thought like that.

Never. Ever.

"Ummm...I'm awake now. So, I'm just going to stay up with Sheldon. Talk to him. Can he hear me?" I asked thinking the safest thing was to talk about Sheldon so that I could remember that I had a husband, albeit an unfaithful one. But I was still married—for now.

"That's something we don't know, but most medical personnel agree that talking to patients who are unconscious is a good thing."

"Then, that's what I'll do. Talk. To...my husband."

"That's wonderful. Because I'm going to give him something that will help him to sleep a little longer than usual."

"Why? Is something wrong with him?"

He shook his head. "No. It's that your husband is a little young to have heart disease. And so we want to make sure that we do everything we can to get his heart as strong as possible. And reduce the chance of another one of these incidents in a few years."

"Is there a chance of that?" I asked.

"None of us ever knows what the future holds, but I'm hoping that by the time your husband leaves here, there will be nothing but healthy hearts all around." He moved toward the door. "I'll be back in a few hours to check on him...and you. Make sure you're both doing well. And when I come back," he paused and looked around at the sterile room, "I'm going to bring a little something to add some Christmas spirit here."

"Thank you," I said.

At the doorway, he paused and turned to me. "There's just a few days till Christmas. What did you ask for?"

I thought about all the things I'd wanted this year: maybe a new tablet, a new phone, a designer purse.

But none of them matched to what I really wanted right here, right now.

I wanted to know who that red thong belonged to.

"Be careful what you ask for," he said before I could even answer. He looked toward the ceiling and pointed. "He'll really give it to you."

I thought about his words—be careful. Was he trying to say that I needed to be careful about finding out who the thong belonged to?

But no...he didn't know what I was thinking.

"Well, it's good to know that God will give us what we ask for, right?" I said.

"As long as it's all in line with His will," he said, sounding way more like a preacher than a doctor. "But many times, people ask for something, not because they have a real desire for it, but because they're asking out of emotions. Emotions should never be the drive behind anyone's requests because emotions can change in an..." He paused and snapped his finger. "In an instant." Before I could ask him what he meant, he said, "Good night, Mrs. Hudson. Sweet dreams."

I stood in place long after he left. Oh yes, I would have sweet dreams tonight. Especially if my dreams were all about Dr. David.

Chapter EIGHT

S avannah."
    I smiled. Though the voice didn't sound the same, I knew who it was. I'd been dreaming about him all night. I opened my eyes, and frowned.

It wasn't the doctor. It was Ginger!

"I wasn't sure if I should wake you," she whispered, "but I brought breakfast." She held up a box of donuts.

Maybe that was how she was going to insure that once Sheldon woke up, he would be hers. Maybe she had laced the donuts with poison. Or maybe, there was nothing but donuts in the box, nothing but sugar and fat that was sure to add on the pounds.

"No. Thank. You."

The way she raised her eyebrows just a little, I could tell that she heard my attitude. But she just shrugged a little.

There was still cheer in her voice when she rested the donut box on the lone table in the room. "I'll just put these down here," she said. "And I also brought over my iPod and speaker. So Sheldon can hear music. Last night I Googled the kinds of things that we could do to help him, and I read that all kinds of stimulation helps: talking, music...."

Did this woman think that she was his wife already? And really, did she plan to just step in like this? While I was right here?

As she pulled the iPod and bluetooth speaker from the small bag, I took in her outfit today—blue jeans, a white turtleneck, Uggs. Red Uggs!

Ugh!

She had dressed down and still looked like she was dressed up.

"I know I don't have to tell you how much Sheldon loves music," she chatted. "Especially his Motown hits."

It hurt; the way she spoke about him with such familiarity. But what hurt more was how good she looked. I could see why my husband chose her, could see why he'd be proud to have her on his arm.

But I wasn't just going to walk away and let her have him. Especially since all of this time, she'd been smiling in my face and skanking behind my back.

Skanking.

I couldn't believe I'd just used one of Theresa's words. According to my best friend, that was a verb that skanks did.

Skanks skanked. And Ginger was definitely a skank who had skanked with my husband.

"There we are!" She stood with her hands on her waist. "All set up."

It was just jeans...and Red Uggs. Why did she look so good?

I took a quick glance down at the sweat pants and T-shirt that I still wore. I really wish that I could say that I threw on this outfit just for the ride to the hospital, but this was what I'd been wearing when Sheldon came home yesterday morning. This was how I'd greeted my husband at the door. After a long trip away, he'd come home to see me dressed-down for real. Sweats and a T-shirt was who I'd become.

I had an excuse though. I hadn't worked outside of our home in years. Not since Sheldon had started that business that he'd dreamed of. His research development firm that specialized in high-end tech products. He started in 1993 right when Intel began shipping the first Pentium chips and everyone knew that big things were ahead. There was talk of smaller computers and smaller cell phones, and even cell phones that would one day act like computers.

And Sheldon's new company was poised to do much of the developmental research for these products that major companies were all racing to introduce by the new millennium.

It was an exciting time, and a profitable one. And a time where Sheldon decided that I didn't need to work outside of our home anymore.

"I want to take care of you," he'd said. "And with you not working, you can raise our wonderful children."

I'd had to remind him that we didn't have any children, but he'd taken care of that, too. I swear it was a year after we had that conversation that the twins were born.

So, I'd had the privilege of being home with our children and being home at night when Sheldon came home from long hours of work. I'd worked hard to provide a comfortable, wonderful place for all three of the people I loved most in the world to lay their heads.

My family had been my career, and I was proud of that. Even once the children were grown, I stayed active with my Sorority and our church.

But with nowhere to go every single day, I didn't have much regard for my daily appearance. Now, I wondered— was that one of the things that Sheldon liked about Ginger over me?

She broke through my thoughts. "I really wish you'd eat something, Savannah."

I wanted to tell her to stop calling me that. Wanted to tell her that I was *Mrs. Hudson* to her and would always be no matter what happened with her and Sheldon.

"I told you...."

She held up her hand. "I get it," she said. "You know, I never used to eat breakfast until Sheldon started bringing breakfast to the office telling me that it was the most important meal of the day.

"But, I was afraid that breakfast would make my hips spread, and I told Sheldon that."

While she laughed at her words, I glared at her. Really? She'd been discussing her hips with my husband?

Not that I had any doubt before, but I had absolutely no doubt about this trick now.

"Now," she continued, "I do eat breakfast, but I have mostly fruit and yogurt." She tilted her head to the side. "I wasn't thinking. That's what I should have brought for you. Do you want me to run out and get you some fruit?"

"No. I'm fine," I said, hardly moving my lips.

"Okay," she said with too much cheer. "And you know what? I was wondering something else, do you think I should call Jon?"

I hadn't thought about Jon. Sheldon's business partner had been in Paris for the last month and he would definitely want to know about Sheldon; he'd have to know.

But there was no way I was going to let Ginger make that call. This was my husband, his business, and she needed to understand that I was going to take care of both.

"I'll...call Jon when the time is right," I said, putting an extra bit of emphasis on the fact that I would do it.

She shrugged. "Okay!"

The way she stood there, all cutesy...I couldn't take it. There was no way I was going to let my husband wake up and see her, then me. I grabbed the hospital telephone, and dialed Theresa's number.

"You good, *Chica*?" Theresa said when she answered the phone.

"How did you know it was me?"

"Howard University Hospital showed up on the Caller ID. Everything good?" she repeated.

"Yeah, I was just wondering if you were going to be coming soon. I wanted to run home and change."

"I can stay here for you," Ginger said, as if I'd invited her to listen in on my conversation.

I ignored her. "Is that all right, Theresa?"

"Of course. I was just getting dressed and was going to call and see if you wanted me to bring you anything."

I glanced over at the box of donuts that Ginger had brought. I wanted one—or three—of those so bad. "No, I'm good," I told her.

"Okay, I'll be there in less than an hour."

The phone was barely back in the cradle before Ginger said, "You don't have to wait for Theresa. I don't mind staying here with Sheldon so that you can go home."

I couldn't do this anymore. This woman was screwing my husband and I was playing nice. For what?

"No, Ginger. In fact, I was going to tell you...." She looked at me with wide brown eyes filled with expectancy. What was it that I was going to tell her? Did I really want to have this showdown right here, right now over my unconscious husband?

"I was going to tell you that a doctor who came to see Sheldon last night asked that we keep his visitors to a minimum. They really only want *family* here."

"Oh," she said, glancing down at Sheldon, then looking up at me.

The way the corners of her lips drooped a little, and the way her wide eyes got smaller, I could almost hear the thought in her head:

But I'm family, too!

And in *my* head, I answered: *No. You're not, heifer. And don't go counting those unhatched chickens.*

She was hurt, but I didn't care. Well, maybe I did care, a little. I'd never been one of those mean girls. So, I added, "It's just that the doctors have given him something that is going to keep him sleeping a little longer than usual for heart patients. They want to give him a little extra time to rest and heal."

"Oh...kay."

"And then, the excitement, and all the stimulation is not always good."

"Oh...kay. I understand," she said, sounding like she didn't understand at all. Then, "So...."

"It's best that you leave now." Those were mean girl words, but I tried to keep my tone more cordial.

"Okay, well." She looked down at Sheldon once again, then back at me as if she hoped that I'd remembered that I once considered her family.

But though I didn't mad-mug her, I kept my expression steady and stern; I was not changing my mind.

"Well," she said as she tugged the strap of her purse onto her arm, "I hope you'll keep me posted."

"I will," I said because I couldn't imagine being so rude as to tell her the truth.

She turned to her iPod on the table, but she didn't pick it up and take it away like I expected. Instead she said, "Do you want me to show you how to work this?"

Inside, I screamed: *Just take it with you*. But the nice girl in me said, "Kym will figure it out." And then because I had been raised so right, I added, "Thank you."

That seemed to make her feel better, even brought back her smile, at least a little.

She came over to the side of the bed where I'd been standing and opened her arms to embrace me. I stiffened when she touched me and she pulled back quickly.

There were all kinds of questions in her eyes, but all she said was, "Okay, I'll be looking to hear from you. And please call me, Savannah, if you need anything. And, I mean that."

I nodded and wondered if she knew that she would never hear from me again. And she wouldn't hear from Sheldon either if I could convince him that he should stay with me—that is, if I convinced myself that I should stay with him.

When she walked out, I pushed the cot to the side, then stood over Sheldon's bed. Being in this room with Sheldon and Ginger and knowing what I knew—the aching in my heart was stronger than any anger. And now, tears burned behind my eyes.

Maybe it was because I hadn't really rested well. Maybe it was because I was so confused. Maybe it was because I loved my husband and I hated that I did.

Whatever it was, it made me cry. And I released every emotion: my hurt, my sadness, my anger.

And then, I cried because I felt so guilty. Sheldon was lying here because of me. I didn't know if that was totally true, since his arteries had such severe blockages. But still, the attack hadn't come until I attacked him.

And if my attack had caused his attack wouldn't I be responsible if he died? I knew his chances of making it were good, but I'd heard of people going into a hospital for a routine procedure and leaving with a one-way ticket to a mortician.

True, he had cheated, but no one should get the death penalty for cheating.

Oh, God! Why had I hit Sheldon? I didn't mean to hurt him. I was just trying to....

"Savannah."

Although it was a whisper, it still startled me. I stood up straight, but couldn't see. My tears were kind of blinding me.

It wasn't until I wiped them away that I saw him. The very fine Dr. David.

"Are you okay, Savannah?"

I nodded and wondered how he knew my name? Last night, he had just called me Mrs. Hudson. But now, we were on a first name basis—I guessed.

As if I'd spoken my question out loud, he said, "Is it all right for me to call you Savannah? I saw your name on the surgical consent form...."

"Yes, of course. That's fine."

"Well, I told you I was going to bring you a little Christmas cheer. How's this?" he asked, holding up the most hideous tree I'd ever seen. It was so bare, looking really like it was just a few sticks that had been stuck together. There were only five or six branches. And it was artificial!

He explained, "You know there can't be any live plants or flowers in the ICU."

I nodded, even though I didn't know that.

"We keep the air as fresh as we can for our patients."

Again I nodded and sniffed back tears.

He looked at me for a long moment, placed the tree on the table and then said, "You look like you could use some fresh air yourself. Walk with me." He stretched out his hand and I just stood there, looking at him.

My hesitation didn't have anything to do with me not wanting to go with this man. It was more about...was it right to be walking around with a doctor when my husband was lying here like this?

Dr. David said, "I'm not asking you out on a date." Then, he chuckled like that had been a joke. "I just want to get you out of this room. You haven't been anywhere except for here, the waiting room, and the chapel since you got here."

How did he know that?

"Let's take a walk," he said again. And before I could protest more, he added, "A short walk."

I glanced at Sheldon; how could a short walk to get some air hurt anything?

"Of course, no one can take care of Sheldon the way you can and you have," he said. "But the nurses will do their best while you're away. And you won't be gone too long." Another pause before he added, "And even if I were to kidnap you and take you away, your daughter and friend will be here soon."

"Okay," I said, having had enough. I planted my hands on my hips. "How do you know that? How do you know all of this?"

He frowned as if he had no idea what I was talking about. "How do you know about my daughter and my friend?"

"Oh," he nodded as if he now understood. "I guess you haven't spent much time in hospitals. Well, one thing you'll learn is that the nurses talk. I heard them talking about you, your daughter, and your friend. They were saying that they could already tell how committed your were to Mr. Hudson. And they said that they wouldn't be concerned when he was released because he'd be in good hands."

Yeah, but would he be in my hands?

Dr. David said, "From what I gathered from the nurses, Mr. Hudson is a very blessed man."

Blessed? That was not a word that I'd heard many doctors use.

"So come on," he said again. "I promise to do you no harm." He smiled and I knew in that instant that this man could never hurt anyone.

"Okay," I said.

He held the door open for me and then with his hand on the small of my back, he led me down the hall to a room with a gold plate on the door: PRIVATE.

I stepped into what felt like a private oasis. Lush plants were in each corner of the room, reminding me a little of that place where Sheldon had taken me all those years ago. Our Adam and Eve fantasy.

And that brought tears to my eyes.

"You don't have to worry," he said, standing in front of me. With the tip of his fingers and a gentle touch, he wiped my tears away. "Your husband is going to be all right. I will do all I can to make sure of that."

"But there's something you don't know." Maybe it was because I was just so weak and tired. Maybe it was because I had been holding it in. But, I blurted out, "It's my fault that he's even here."

"No, it's not."

I nodded.

He said, "You don't have that kind of power." With just a slight glance at the ceiling, he added, "Only He does."

"But, I was...I was..." I fell back onto one of the oversized chairs. And the soft fabric felt like it hugged my frame. "I got upset because I asked Sheldon a question and he wouldn't answer me. I had just wanted him to answer me." Then, I pressed my lips together. Because I was afraid that I'd say more, having already said too much; I certainly didn't want him to know what the argument had been about.

He was so gentle, so caring when he said, "You didn't cause this. And frankly, neither did the Lord. But He is sovereign. The One who allows it all to happen. The One who is in control. We just have to pray for His will to happen."

"But why did He allow this to happen?"

Dr. David shrugged. "Those are the questions that we won't be able to answer, at least not in this life. We will never be able to understand an infinite God with our finite minds."

I sniffed.

Dr. David continued, "Let me ask you this...if Mr. Hudson had answered your question, would you have believed him?"

I looked up. It almost sounded as if he knew what my question had been. Had I said something, had I told him without even realizing it?

Then he asked, "Or would you have continued to question him until he satisfied what you believed to be true?"

"I...don't know." I paused to think about his question, feeling confused. I said, "I don't even know what's true anymore."

"Yes, you do, Savannah. You know the truth and you know where to go to find the truth."

"What do you mean?"

This time, he didn't answer me with words. He just did that thing that he always seemed to do—he glanced up at the ceiling.

I wanted him to answer me, but he said, "It's time to go back to your husband. Your daughter is there."

"How do you know that?"

"I'm just sure she's there by now." He reached for my hand just like he'd done before.

When I stood, I felt almost...refreshed. I didn't have not a single answer, but I didn't feel weighed down with so many questions.

As we walked down the hall, he whispered, "Remember, God has had such a hand on your life. He would've never brought you this far to leave you now."

I tilted my head up. Was this man really a doctor of science?

He pushed open the door to Sheldon's room, and just like Dr. David said, there was Kym.

She looked up as we stepped in. "Mother, I was getting worried."

"Why?" I said, as I pulled my daughter into an embrace. "Because you weren't here and at first, I thought that you'd gone to the bathroom, but the nurses said they didn't see you leave. Where were you?"

"Oh, I was with," I turned around to introduce Kym to Dr. David. But he wasn't behind me. He hadn't come into the room.

"You were with who?" Kym asked.

I frowned, but then, I shook my head. He probably had been called away while I was hugging Kym. "I was with Doctor David. He wanted me to talk to me about a few things."

"About Daddy?"

"Kind of."

"Kind of? Is Daddy going to be all right?"

"Oh, yes, sweetheart. He is."

She nodded like she was going to hold me to that promise. "Well, I thought you said you were going to call me if you needed anything."

"I didn't need anything."

"But Aunt Resa called me and said that you called her. She's on her way, but she wanted me to get here, too."

"I only called her so that I could change my clothes. But, I was going to call you."

She looked at me as if she had major doubts about that. But once she took her attention away from me, her voice softened, "How's Daddy?"

"The doctor said he's coming along."

"I wonder why he hasn't woken up yet?"

"Oh, the doctor told me last night." And then, I explained to her what Dr. David said about the importance of extended rest for Sheldon. "I think it's great because this is all about healing and rest for your father."

"That makes sense," she said as she stood at the side of the bed. "Still, I wish...."

I squeezed her hand for extra assurance. "Your dad is going to be fine. The worst is behind him; he survived the surgery."

"I know. But I Googled last night and found out all the things that could still go wrong after heart surgery."

As my daughter rattled off all kinds of things, like lung and kidney failure, infections, blood loss and blood clots, I shook my head. Did they all go home and look this up on the Internet?

I stood by my daughter's side, looking down at her father.

"I promise you, Kym, none of those things will happen to your father."

It was a promise that I hoped I could keep.

She nodded, but kept her eyes on Sheldon. "I spoke to Kyle this morning."

"Oh, I didn't even think about calling him back."

"I forgot, too. I got back to my apartment, and started working on finishing my application for Doctors Without Borders...."

"Oh, that's right," I said. "How's that coming along?"

"Good, I have to have it done in a couple of days. Before Christmas. But I was too tired to work on it last night. After hanging out on the Internet for a little while, I just fell into bed; I was so tired. But my phone rang at about four this morning. I guess Kyle couldn't take it anymore. He was already trying to get on a flight to come home." She turned to me. "But he can't come yet because he has a problem with his passport."

I frowned.

She said, "He couldn't find it."

I inhaled. Kyle had been like that since he was born. He could never find anything: his shoes, his keys, once, he was even sure that he'd lost his car at the mall.

"And since today is Sunday, he can't go to the Consulate, but he said he'll handle it tomorrow. He said he called your phone, but I told him that yours was at home and Daddy's was dead."

"Okay, I'll give him a call." I paused. "Maybe he shouldn't come home since your father is better now."

After a moment's pause, Kym said, "That's what I was thinking. You know how much he wants to finish this documentary."

"I'll call him and talk to him."

"Okay, but I'm not sure you'll be able to keep him away. He really wants to be here with you."

Those words warmed me up. I wanted Kyle to be here, but I knew Sheldon would be disappointed if he cost Kyle this opportunity. Our son wanted to be a filmmaker and a newsmaker. This was a chance that not many college students ever had.

"*¿Qué pasa gente,*" Theresa strolled into the room as if this wasn't the ICU.

"*No hay mucho,*" Kym replied.

"Uh...." I waved my hand and Theresa chuckled. "You know how I get," she said, resting her coat on a chair. Then, she stepped over to me. She gave me a hug before she lifted Sheldon's hand.

Leaning over, she said, "*Que te mejores pronto, mi amigo.*" When she looked up, it must've been the look on my face that made her laugh. "I'm talking dirty to your husband, *Chica.*"

I frowned. Any other time, that might have been funny. But today?

"No, really," Theresa said. "I read on the Internet last night that speaking in other languages can help to stimulate the brain if a patient is unconscious."

Oh! Lord!

"So, what did you say to him?"

She squinted her eyes and pouted like she was really studying me. "You don't think I was *really* talking dirty, do you? You know, me don't do no skanking. And with someone else's husband, my best friend's husband? That would be skanking to the tenth degree! *No mamie. No sucediendo aquí.* I was just kidding." She wiggled her finger back and forth in a that-is-not-happening-here motion.

And for the first time since this had happened, I laughed. And I really hoped that Sheldon could hear me.

Chapter NINE

There was only one reason why I was in this car. It was because my best friend had taken to calling me names.

"Vannie, you look like a vampire!"

That's what she said to me right after we'd had that laugh about talking dirty to Sheldon and she finally told me that she'd only asked him to get well soon.

"A vampire? Really? Gee...thanks."

"I'm just keeping it one-hundred, *Chica*. So, you ready to break out of here and go home?"

"No, I'm good. I don't want to leave."

"Wait! What?" She looked like I was the one now speaking Spanish. "Didn't you just call me and ask me to come here so that you could go home?"

I'd already forgotten about that call. Mostly, I'd called Theresa as a kind of passive-aggressive move to handle Ginger. "Yeah, but I'm good now."

"No. You're not," Theresa said, folding her arms.

"I agree with Aunt Resa," Kym said. "It really helped me when I went home last night. And you sent us home so that we could do this in shifts, right? So it's your turn to rest."

"But really, I'm good."

Kym and Theresa exchanged a glance and then the two of them pressed their lips together and folded their arms. It looked like Kym had a new twin.

"What?" I asked.

"You. Look," Theresa started.

"A. Hot. Mess," Kym finished as if the two had rehearsed that.

Then, Theresa just had to drive home the insults some more with, "You've got to go home because you cannot be telling people that you're my girl, looking like a vampire."

"Would you stop with the name-calling? I don't want to leave Sheldon alone. Suppose he wakes up? Plus, you know me. If I go home I'm not going to rest anyway."

"Fine. Then, you can come right back. But at least you won't be a smelly vampire anymore."

"Really, Theresa," I said, not feeling her jokes. Especially since I wasn't sure she was kidding since her lips didn't turn into any kind of a smile while she teased me.

"And I don't get what you mean about you don't want to leave Daddy alone," Kym said, jumping in. "What's wrong with me?"

Now, *she* was upset?

My daughter said, "Daddy won't be alone if I'm here, Mother. I'll stay until you get back." She turned to Theresa and told her, "You go with her," as if she were in charge. "At least you can make her lay down for a little while since you said she looks like a zombie."

Theresa raised her eyebrows. "I didn't say zombie, I said vampire. If you are going to be my doctor, you are going to have to pay attention to details."

"Well okay, but if you are going to say she looks like something, then you need to know the difference between a vampire and a zombie. She looks like a zombie."

Then, they both stared at me with straight faces.

"Really?" I said, kind of pissed.

A couple of seconds ticked by and then the both of them burst out laughing. Clearly, I didn't find any of this funny. But I wasn't in the mood for all of this name calling, so I agreed to go home.

So now here I was, in Theresa's car. And once we pulled into the driveway, I had to admit, I was really glad to have my best friend as my escort. Because I never considered what it would be like to walk back into this house for the first time after what happened to Sheldon.

I needed my friend, my backbone with me.

I took a deep breath as I slid out of Theresa's car, and then inhaled another when I put my key in the door.

When I stepped inside, I paused for a moment thinking that so much had happened since I'd left yesterday morning. It felt a lot more like a lifetime rather than just a little over a day. But that's all it had been. Only about twenty-six hours.

And though I felt so much had changed in my life, my home looked exactly the same. Except for the little clues that had been left behind: the scratch on the wall at the bottom of the staircase where the EMTs had struggled just a little with the stretcher that carried Sheldon, my cell phone that rested on the table in the foyer where I'd left it.

"Are you all right?" Theresa whispered.

That quickly, I'd forgotten that she was with me. "I'm fine," I said, though now, I regretted having her here. Would there be signs in the bedroom of what happened? Of how I had attacked Sheldon?

She said, "I'm going to make you some tea while you go take a shower, okay?"

I didn't look at her because my friend had a way of being able to see my thoughts. So, I just nodded and hurried up the stairs to my bedroom. At the door, I paused again.

The towel was still on the floor, right next to the thong.

The thong!

Thank God Theresa was downstairs. She would've guessed something, knowing that I was not the type of girl to wear a thong.

I grabbed the thong and wrapped it inside the towel, then stuffed the bundle into the trashcan. Then, I turned to Sheldon's suitcase that was still on the edge of the bed. As I zipped it, I stopped for a moment; the conversation that I had with him right before he got on the red-eye on Friday night came to my mind....

The ringing phone jolted me from my sleep and I answered, trying to keep my grogginess out of my voice.

"Hello, beautiful," he said.

"Hi."

"I'm so sorry to wake you, but I didn't want to get on this plane without hearing your voice."

"Is your flight taking off on time?"

"It better be. I was running a little behind and had to have the cab act like a speed racer in order to get here, but I'm at the gate now and we're starting to board."

"Oh, why were you running late?"

"Last minute business," he said. "But even if I had missed the flight, I was leaving tonight. I would've chartered my own jet, just to get home to you."

Now, Sheldon had me fully awake. After all these years, he still made me tingle.

He said, "So, I'll see you in the morning. You'll be ready for me?"

"That's why I went to bed early. I want to make sure that I'm ready."

He chuckled, but then, his tone turned serious. "I love you, Savannah. With all of my heart...."

I'd felt wonderful when I laid the phone down, having no idea that my husband was lying. He'd probably had to rush to his plane because he didn't want to leave Ginger as she paraded around in her thong and pencil heels.

Of course, she wore nothing else. No need, her breasts were still perky, sitting up high because she'd yet to have children.

That image had me wound up again and with both hands, I carried his suitcase to the closet and tossed it inside. It hit the floor with a thump and I slammed his door shut.

Now, everything was out of sight, but not out of my mind. The red thong, the red stilettos, and Ginger.

"Here's your tea," Theresa said, interrupting my descent into depression.

With unsteady hands, I took the cup from her, but I shook so much that Theresa hurried to take it away from me. She placed the cup on the nightstand, then held my hand and led me to the bed.

"You don't have to be strong around me. I'm your girl." She wrapped me into an embrace and held me tight.

I was not going to cry, even though I wanted to. But why would I be crying? Because I was sad or because I was mad? I just didn't know.

Theresa leaned back and the way she looked at me, I knew she expected tears. I just had none to give.

"You can cry," she encouraged. "It's okay; I'm here for you."

"I know. I guess I'm just too tired. Maybe I will stay here for a little while and rest."

That was supposed to be a clue. She could go home because after that little memory, I wanted so bad to be by myself.

But all she did was nod.

So, I added, "I just need some time alone." That was a little more than a hint. Because I didn't want to just come out and say, 'Go home.' My goal wasn't to hurt her feelings. My goal was to wallow in my misery alone.

"Okay. Well, you shower and then rest. I'll entertain myself downstairs." She grasped my hands inside of hers. "I know it has to be hard to sit and watch the man that you love fight for his life. But that's the key word—Sheldon is fighting. Because he loves you. And that alone is a blessing. You have something that I really didn't think existed—you have a really good man. God blessed you; He gave you a true love and He's not about to take that away."

This was where I should have told her that my blessing had twisted into a curse.

She said, "And you know what, *Chica*? Because of you and Sheldon, I now believe that one day this can happen for me."

This was where I should have told her that she'd been right all along—all men were dogs!

"That's my dream," she added.

But now I couldn't tell her any of that. Because now, she had a dream. And I didn't want to take that away from her. She'd find out about Sheldon soon enough.

So I just hugged her and thanked her and nodded my head when she told me that she'd be downstairs if I needed her.

I didn't have any choice—she was going to stay. That was just like my life right now. I didn't have too much of a choice in anything.

Chapter
TEN

I had stayed away too long and I couldn't believe it.

I'd taken a shower and then finally fallen into a fitful sleep somewhere around eleven. My plan was to only take a short nap until about noon or maybe one at the latest.

But I'd slept and slept and slept. Until I rolled over and wondered why my bedroom was so dark. I had my answer when I glanced at the clock.

It was after six! How in the world had I slept so long? And why didn't Theresa wake me?

She must have gone home. But when I ran downstairs to check, she was in the living room, kicked back on the sofa with her feet tucked beneath her, watching television.

She looked up when I stepped into the room. "Oh, you're up, *Chica!*"

"Why didn't you wake me?"

"Because you needed to get some rest."

"But I need to be at the hospital. Kym has been there all this time by herself."

"Well, actually," Theresa said as she straightened up, "Kym called. She left about three; she was checking to see if you were on your way back because she wanted to get back home and work on her application for Doctors Without Borders." She paused. "I am so proud of that girl!"

"So, she left Sheldon alone?" I couldn't believe that. Kym would never leave her father.

Theresa frowned. "He's not alone. He's being watched very carefully by the doctors and nurses there."

I was already halfway back up the steps when I said, "I've got to get dressed. I've got to get back to him."

The entire time I dressed, I wondered why was I rushing to be with Sheldon? Why did I care...why would I care if Sheldon was alone; after what he'd done, I was the one feeling lonely.

I guess love died hard. And I *was* his wife. I took my vows seriously, even if he didn't. I was going to perform all my duties fully until he got well. Then, I would file for divorce.

I paused. Divorce.

For the first time that was a serious thought. Did I really want to divorce Sheldon? Did I not want to fight for him?

Those questions, my thoughts, everything was just too complicated for me right now, so I kept my focus on getting back to the hospital.

Within thirty minutes of waking up, we were back in Theresa's car, both silent as we rode. At least ten minutes passed before Theresa said, "You're so quiet."

I kept my eyes on the shops and restaurants that lined 7th Street as we edged through the Sunday evening traffic in Chinatown. "I have a lot on my mind."

After a moment, she said, "Anything you want to talk about?"

There was lots that I wanted to talk about. But nothing that I could talk about with her. At least, not yet. I'd have to tell her everything once I left Sheldon. And in a way, I couldn't wait. I was counting on my friend, who'd been through so many divorces, to help me make it through mine.

But I wasn't ready to go there with her yet, so I just shrugged and hoped that would be enough.

It wasn't. She said, "Vannie, you do know you can talk to me about anything, right?"

"Yes."

Then, she stayed quiet until she stopped the car in front of the hospital's entrance.

"I'll be back in a couple of hours," she said. "I'll take you home tonight."

"No, that's okay. I'm going to spend the night."

"Again? Why? You shouldn't do that; you should," and then, she stopped.

We were friends because while we were so very different, we shared some common traits—including our stubbornness. She knew she wouldn't be able to convince me to leave. Especially not after I'd stayed away for so long today.

So, Theresa just finished with, "I'll come back to check on you."

"Thank you," I said for so many reasons.

I rushed into hospital, checked in with the Information Desk, got my pass, then made my way up to the cardiac ICU. The nurses who'd been on night duty last night greeted me right before I stepped into Sheldon's room. I laid my coat on the chair, before I moved as quietly as I could to his bed.

Not that it mattered; he was still asleep.

Even though Dr. David told me that he would be sleep a little longer than normal, I didn't feel good about this. It couldn't be good for someone to still be unconscious even after twenty-four hours, could it?

I glanced at the iPod that Ginger had left on the table. And for a moment, I thought about turning it on. But then, why should I use anything that came from Ginger? The best music would come from me. The best music would be my voice.

So, I leaned over the rail. And putting my lips close to Sheldon's ear, I whispered, "Sheldon, this is Savannah." I paused. What else was I supposed to say? Should I tell him that I loved him or that I hated him?

I said neither. Just, "I want you to get well, Sheldon. I really do. But then, where are we going to go from here? What am I supposed to do when I don't even know why you cheated or if you still love me."

I paused as if I were waiting for Sheldon to miraculously sit up and tell me all that I needed to know.

And then...a miracle!

His eyes fluttered, then opened. Not all the way, but enough for me to see.

"Sheldon!" I said. I ignored the joy that I heard in my voice. "You're awake. Thank God!"

He just stared at me. His lips moved, but no sound came out. And then, he lifted his hand and touched mine.

"Thank God, you're all right. Let me call the nurse."

But before I could move, his eyes closed.

"Sheldon!" I shouted.

Fear filled me; but then, his chest was still moving. Up. Down. He was breathing; he was alive.

"Please come back," I whispered. "Please wake up again. I need you to be well." I paused. "And, I need...answers."

"Good evening."

Looking up, my glance fell on Dr. David and that gleaming smile that he carried.

I ignored that smile, and his looks, and the way he made me feel safe and so secure with just his presence. I asked, "Is this normal?"

"What?"

"Sheldon opened his eyes, but it was for only a minute. And now, he's asleep again. Is that normal?"

"Life is as normal as God wants it to be," he said as he checked the chart at the end of Sheldon's bed.

Why was this man talking in riddles? He just needed to answer my question and tell me what I needed to know.

As if he knew what I was thinking, Dr. David put down the chart and said, "Remember, I told you that he would be asleep for longer than usual."

"Yes, but I just told you, he woke up."

"He wasn't really awake," the doctor said. "That was a reflex. He's still asleep and he needs this time to heal completely. He needs this time...and so do you." A pause, and then, "Walk with me."

Again? I said inside. But on the outside, I just glanced at Sheldon and then followed the doctor.

Why did I keep doing this? Every time Dr. David told me to go with him, I did. I guess it had to be because I was just so curious about this man.

"Where are we going?" I asked.

"Just to get a cup of coffee." Then a second later, he added, "Wait, you prefer tea, right?"

I glanced up at him. "How did you know that?"

He gave me that smile that was brighter than sunshine. "You just seem like you would be a tea drinker."

"Yeah, okay," I said, wondering what this man's game was. I mean, I knew he was Sheldon's doctor, but he seemed to be taking so much of a special interest in me.

As we passed by the Nurses' station, one of the nurses said, "Going to take a little break, Mrs. Hudson?"

I nodded. "We're going to the cafeteria."

When I looked up at Dr. David, the nurse frowned. "Okay," she said slowly. "I'll check on Mr. Hudson until you get back."

"Thank you."

Inside the elevator, I said, "It's interesting how you have time for these little breaks all the time. Don't you have other patients?"

"Sometimes it feels like I have millions of them."

It was not only his words that made me laugh, but the way he said them. As if he were serious.

But I guess his words weren't meant to be funny because without a smile on his face nor in his tone, he said, "But right now, I don't have a patient who is as important as you."

"You mean my husband, don't you?"

"Yes, I'm here for you...your husband, of course." And then, that smile was back, making my heart take just a little extra beat.

That hadn't happened to me...since Sheldon and I first started dating.

Inside the cafeteria, he walked me to a table first, then said, "I'll get our tea. Milk and Equal for you?"

I frowned.

He held up his hand before I could ask him how did he know? He said, "I'm a doctor; I'm supposed to be able to deduce certain things. Or what kind of physician would I be?"

As he moved toward the station that held the coffee and the tea, I watched him. There was something about this man. Yes, he was fine, the kind of fine that made it difficult to move your eyes away from him. The kind of fine that I knew even Theresa wouldn't be able to resist. The kind of fine that only appeared in movies and best-selling novels.

But he was so much more than that. First, there were his words. Though sometimes confusing, they were always soothing. And he was smooth, so smooth. Even the way he walked—like he was traveling on clouds.

And then, his presence...what could I say about that? Except that I now knew why I always said yes to him—I just wanted to be near him, to see him, hear him...touch him and have him touch me!

"Stop it!" I whispered, and reeled myself back in. What was I thinking? Did I have a thing for Sheldon's doctor?

I couldn't have. I was a married woman and never in the twenty-three years of our marriage did I ever look at another man.

Of course, that was before I found out that Sheldon had been looking at another woman.

I shook my head, hoping that would rattle those thoughts away. No matter what Sheldon had done, I couldn't cheat on him. That just wasn't in me. I would never be able to lay my head down at night if I did what Sheldon had been doing.

"I hope you like your tea. I selected the decaffeinated green tea, since it's getting late."

Even when he sat the cup in front of me, I didn't look up. He seemed to know all of this stuff—and I wanted a clear head before I set my eyes on him and he looked into mine.

Because if he could somehow read minds, he would know what I'd been thinking....

I lifted the cup to my lips, waited a second, and then sipped the hot liquid. Perfect.

Now, I looked up and at him. Dr. David winked and smirked like he was confident that he had gotten it right.

My thoughts swerved to the left again; to what I could only think of as "The Temptation Zone".

And I was all up in that zone. I started thinking that it was clear the doctor had a thing for me. And Sheldon had already cheated. And maybe I would feel better if I did to Sheldon what he'd done to me.

"Do you know that rest is very important when one is healing?" he said.

"What?" I asked, wondering what he was talking about. Had I missed something while I was sitting here imagining what it would be like to be in bed with him?

He said, "Rest. It's so important to healing. That's why I'm going to make sure that your husband sleeps for a while." He paused. "And rest, is so important in life. It's when people are tired that they're the most vulnerable, most open to temptation."

Temptation?

No way!

It wasn't really possible for anyone to read another person's mind, was it? Of course not. But still, I wanted to drill a hole into the floor so that I could disappear.

But I wasn't going to let him see just how embarrassed I was. I said, "I understand now. It's important for Sheldon's heart," hoping to direct the conversation and my thoughts back to my husband.

"Rest is needed for anybody dealing with heart issues. Both of you need it."

"Oh, I'm fine." I waved his words away. "Just worried about Sheldon."

"No need to worried about him. His operation fixed his heart issues. Yours on the other hand...." He stopped as if I understood.

"What are you talking about? There's nothing wrong with me...or my heart."

"Well, I wouldn't say that. You may not need the surgery your husband needed, but you do need time to relax and reflect. I know this has been hard on you."

Oh! He was only talking about my stress from Sheldon's heart attack.

"This has been stressful," I told him, "but I don't need to relax too much, nor do too much reflecting." I took another sip of tea. "You know what the Bible says about an idle mind—it's the devil's workshop."

"True." He nodded. "But one thing we both know; your mind is not idle. There's a lot going on," he leaned across the table and tapped his forefinger gently against my temple, "in there," he said, sitting back in his chair. "We just need to make sure that you're focused on the right things."

I hardly heard what he'd said after he'd touched me. All I wanted to do was lift my hand and feel where his finger had been.

He said, "Your thoughts have to be right and in-line with God and what He has planned for you."

With God.

I couldn't really think about what God had planned for me when I didn't think He'd done a good job with this whole situation. Not only had He allowed Sheldon to cheat on me, but whenever I asked God, "Why?" all He ever said was *No.*

Dr. David crossed his arms on the table and leaned forward. "There is one thing that I know about God. He always hears us, even when we think He doesn't. And He's always answering, even when we think He's not."

Well, I knew for sure that wasn't true. Because God wasn't answering my question. And just to make sure, while Dr. David sat there talking, inside I asked God again:

Why did Sheldon cheat on me?

No.

See what I mean?

Dr. David said, "So, you can go to Him and talk to Him any time you want to. And here on earth, you can always talk to me. I know we haven't known each other long...."

Long? We hadn't even known each other for twenty-four hours.

He continued, "But I think we have a connection."

So...it wasn't just me. He did feel it, too.

"And, there's always a reason why God puts people in your life."

A reason.

Maybe that was the reason why Dr. David became Sheldon's doctor. So that I could have someone to talk to. So that I could get a man's perspective, get an understanding of why men, who claimed to be happily married, would cheat—since God wasn't giving me the answer.

But just as quickly as I opened my mouth to ask those questions, I pressed my lips back together. This man, though kind, though fine, was nothing more than a stranger. I couldn't get this comfortable, this intimate with someone I didn't know.

"You don't have to say anything now," he said as if he saw my doubts. "Just know that I'm here if you do need to talk.

I nodded.

"Good." Then, he leaned back and changed the subject. "So you're not going to stay here tonight, are you? You can go home and sleep in your own bed."

"I went home this morning and I just got back. Right before you came into the room."

"Oh, I didn't know that," he said.

I don't know why that made me feel better. He *didn't* know everything.

"Well, I still think it would be best for you to rest at home."

I shook my head. "I want to be here...in case Sheldon wakes up again. And, I really hate leaving him alone."

He brightened the room again, showing all thirty-two of his pearly whites. "You do know that he won't be alone; he's never alone."

"I know that, but I'm his wife."

He nodded. "That you are. So let me get you back to his room."

He took my cup and his, tossed them into the trashcan, then led me from the cafeteria.

"I hope that was a good break for you," he said.

I smiled when I looked up at him. "It was. It really was."

On the third floor, the elevator doors parted, and we stepped out. Just a few feet away, Theresa stood, chatting with one of the nurses.

"There you are," Theresa said coming toward me. "She was just telling me that you took a break."

"Yeah," I said. "We went to the cafeteria. Oh, let me introduce you. Theresa, this is," I turned around.

And Dr. David was gone.

Chapter
ELEVEN

S avannah."
    I heard the soft whisper of my name and I didn't want to open my eyes. It felt like I had just closed them. But then, when I heard my name once again, I opened my eyes with a sigh.

"I'm so sorry to wake you, dear."

I looked up into the eyes of Mrs. Martin, the First Lady of Church of the Nazarene, the church that Sheldon and I attended.

"Oh," I said, softly swinging my legs onto the floor. That was when I saw Pastor Martin standing across the room, at the foot of Sheldon's bed.

"Is everything all right?" I asked, jumping up.

Had something happened to Sheldon during the night and they'd called our pastor?

"Everything is fine, dear," First Lady Martin said, putting a calming hand on my shoulder. "We just came this morning, as soon as we heard. Why didn't you call and tell us?"

"I'm sorry. I just didn't think about it. I almost forgot to call Kym and Kyle."

"Well, that's okay, dear." She patted my hand. "We're here now."

"Yes, we are! We're here to stand with and pray for you." Pastor Martin's voice boomed, filling up the room, exactly the way he filled the sanctuary on Sundays.

I stretched my neck, leaning first to the right, then the left. "Thank you," I said.

First Lady Martin stepped away from me, and stood by her husband's side. Although it was Monday morning, you would never be able to tell it by these two.

Mrs. Martin was dressed in a bright red knit suit with a skirt that hung down to her ankles. And atop her head, she wore a green hat with ribbons and rhinestones that was so tall, it added at least two inches to her height. Pastor Martin wore a green suit that matched his wife's hat. And his red tie was as bright as her suit.

I was thinking that if I had each of them hold up a couple of bulbs, they'd look just like a Christmas tree.

"Have you been here by yourself?" the First Lady asked, taking my thoughts away from their outfits.

I shook my head. "No, my friend Theresa was here until almost midnight, but she had to leave to get up for work today. I think Kym will be here soon."

"That's good," she said. "But maybe you should have gone home last night, too. That cot looks terribly uncomfortable." She scrunched her nose and shook her head like she disapproved.

"No, I was good. I wanted to stay. I had to stay because Sheldon woke up yesterday."

"Did he?"

I nodded. "And, I wanted to be here if he woke up again."

"So, he's recovering well?" Pastor Martin asked as he looked down at Sheldon.

"The doctors say that he is."

First Lady Martin raised her hands toward heaven. "Thank. You. Lord." Looking back at me, she said, "You know we think of you and Sheldon as our spiritual son and daughter."

I nodded.

"Yes," Pastor added. "Sheldon's father and I," he paused and waved his hand, "well, you know the story. But I promised my buddy when he was on his death bed that I would look after you and Sheldon. And I take that responsibility seriously."

I knew that they did. Sheldon and I were both only children who'd lost our parents: Me, before Sheldon and I were married, and him after.

The Martins had stepped in as surrogates, which had always been a blessing to us, especially for Kym and Kyle who saw them as grandparents.

Pastor Martin moved to one side of the bed and took Sheldon's hand. The First Lady came to me and took mine. And then, the pastor did what he did best—he took our concerns and our requests to the Lord.

"Let us bow our heads," he said as if we needed that instruction. "Lord, we come to You today with open and grateful hearts...."

I closed my eyes and tried to stay in the prayer, paying attention to every word. But it was difficult to stay focused. Because every single time I thought about God, I thought about the question that He had yet to answer—why, why, why? Why did He let Sheldon cheat?

I mean, I understood that we all had free will and everything, but hadn't God put any kind of conviction on Sheldon's heart? Hadn't God reminded Sheldon that he loved me and that I would be so hurt once this all came out?

Maybe this was a good time for me to ask God again. While I stood under the anointing of this prayer and so close to this man and woman of God. Maybe now God would hear my question and give me an answer.

As Pastor Martin prayed aloud, I prayed inside.

God, why did Sheldon cheat?

No.

I just wanted to scream. What was wrong? Why wouldn't God answer me?

I didn't ask again. I just stood with my head bowed until Pastor Martin said, "Amen."

After the prayer, the Martins sat with me for much longer than I wanted. I wanted to be alone with Sheldon; I needed to be, just in case he awakened. Just in case he opened his eyes, and called Ginger's name.

No one else would know what that meant. But if he did that to me, I was going to unplug his breathing tube.

But finally, Pastor Martin pushed back his chair. "Well, it's time for us to go," he said.

"Thank you for coming."

"We wouldn't have it any other way, dear." The First Lady pulled me into a bear hug, almost suffocating me against her ample breasts. When she leaned away, she said, "You're blessed, Savannah. In fact, we are all blessed to have this man of God, this upright man, this good man." She glanced over at Sheldon, still laying in his peaceful sleep. "A man who will one day stand before God and hear, 'Well done.' But, I don't want you to worry. That day is not now. His time has not yet come." She held my shoulders. "You hear me, don't you?"

I nodded and faked a smile. Yeah, I'd heard her. Talking about how good and wonderful Sheldon was. I just wanted to blurt out the truth to everyone. Tell them all Sheldon's secret. What would Pastor and First Lady Martin think if they knew that one of their deacons was nothing more than a dog?

But, I played the good wife as I hugged them and said nothing more than goodbye.

The world would know about Sheldon Hudson soon enough. But first, he needed to wake up and answer my questions. Since God wouldn't do it.

Chapter
TWELVE

I had really wanted to stay at the hospital. But as the hours passed on Monday, I knew that I was just too tired to face another night on that cot.

First Lady Martin had been right this morning when she said the cot looked uncomfortable. It was and it had left me stiff all day.

So I'd done the only thing that I could; I'd come home.

"Are you sure you're going to be all right, Mother?" Kym said as she sat in the driveway of our home.

"Of course. I've stayed here alone before. Many times, as your father traveled."

"I know that. It's just that this is different." She stopped and thought for a moment. "If you won't let me stay with you, maybe I should call Aunt Resa."

"Maybe you should just go home." I leaned over and kissed her cheek. "You can call me before you go to sleep and first thing in the morning, all right?"

She hugged me back. "All right, Mommy."

I slid out of the car and then trotted up the steps, turning to wave to Kym before I stepped inside and closed the door.

Through the window, I watched Kym back her car out of the driveway, then turn up the street. I sighed. It was good to be alone and away from watchful eyes.

After Pastor Martin and his wife left, I thought I was free. But Kym had shown up less than fifteen minutes later and she never left. Even though she hadn't finished her Doctors Without Borders application, and I kept telling her to go home, go to the library, go wherever and work on it, she'd stayed with me. She never left, not even when Theresa came strolling into the hospital after her long day of teaching first graders.

Finally, I'd left so that Kym would, too. And so that I could have a little peace.

Turning around, I flipped on the light and in an instant, all kinds of memories flooded my mind. Every corner of this room held a fragrance of our love. Or at least the love I thought we'd had.

I dropped my purse by the table and went over to the leather recliner that was Sheldon's favorite.

Leaning back, I closed my eyes and wallowed in the good times. From when we first married and how we played this game where we picked a different place in the house to have sex. The game wouldn't end until we'd covered at least one place in every room. It never took us very long to play, just a few hours because we were non-stop.

Back then.

Sex now was not like it was then. Is that what Sheldon was looking for? Is that why Sheldon had strayed? It wasn't totally my fault that we weren't like rabbits anymore. Life happened, we were older.

But Ginger was not older, and I imagined Sheldon playing the game with her now—at her home, or his car, or in some hotel room. Oh, and let me not forget, the office. That was where the two of them spent most of their time.

He was probably popping those little blue pills for her as she popped her booty for him.

I shuddered. After the way I'd loved this man, after all that I'd put into him, there was no way that I would ever trust another one.

I was going to join the Theresa Perez All-Men-Are-Dogs Club.

Right when I had that thought, an image of Dr. David's face filled my mind. Now, a man like him would *never* cheat. He would love, honor and cherish, the way God intended... and the way Sheldon had promised.

I reclined the lounger back further until I was almost at ninety-degrees. And then, my mind faded back to another time, a different day. To our last birthday. The party that celebrated our 47th birthdays....

"Shake it fast, watch yourself, shake it fast, show 'em what you working with."

The music blared through the speakers that Kyle had set up since he was DJ'ing this party. Like all of the parties that we had to make merry on our shared birthdays, our living room was filled with friends, mostly from our church.

Kym screamed, "Let's get this party started." She sashayed her way over to me. "Show 'em what you're working with, Mother! Show 'em."

What in the world was I supposed to do?

But then, Theresa took over. Even though she had on a halter dress that ended mid-thigh, she raised her hands high above her head, and shook her booty—fast.

"Go 'head, Aunt Resa!" Kym squealed.

Even Sheldon had joined in. Doing some kind of move, though he and the beat never seemed to find each other. But that didn't stop our friends from cheering him on.

Sheldon reached out his hand to me and I had no choice. I took it...and then, I showed everyone what I was working with.

My daughter, who just moments before was cheering me on, frowned like she was appalled.

"Mother, what are you doing?"

"I'm shaking it fast." I had never been the best dancer in any room. But whatever I was doing was definitely better than Sheldon.

Kym laughed. "Kyle, look at your Mother."

Sheldon and I ignored our children, and even the cheers of our friends. It was just the two of us, the way it always was.

I was exhausted when Sheldon finally pulled me into his arms and slowed it down, even though "Shake it Fast" still played.

"You know why I love you so much?" he asked.

"Why?" I looked into his eyes as he kissed me on my nose.

"Because I get to live out all of my dreams with you." He kissed my forehead. "There is nothing else in this world that I long for more than you." He kissed my right cheek. "And what's so wonderful?" He kissed my left cheek. "Is that I already know that tomorrow, I'll love you more than today."

It was a good thing that Sheldon was holding me because when he kissed my lips, I thought I would wilt right then and end up as a pile of mush in the middle of our party.

When our lips finally unlocked, we were both breathless, but my husband still had more to say.

He whispered, "Everything that I've hoped for, everything that I've ever wanted happens because of you. You're the part of me that...."

"Kyle!" Kym shouted over her father's words. "Play something mushy to go with all of this mushy stuff that Daddy is saying to Mother." She was still cracking up when she turned back to us. "This is your birthday party, not your anniversary party."

"Yeah," Theresa chimed in. "And, you have guests. You keep that up and we'll all have to go home. Or maybe, we'll just make

the two of you leave so you can get a hotel room somewhere. No estoy bromeando."

The room erupted in laughter, but Sheldon still held me as we swayed to a beat that was only in our heads.

Sheldon said, "Don't hate on me because I love my wife."

More laughter, more music, more fun...and more love. Especially, when our son played our song....

I believe in you and me...

I believe that we will be...

In love eternally...

I opened my eyes slowly, not really wanting to leave that day behind. That wonderful day just three months ago. It had been Fall then, but now it was Winter...in so many ways.

The pain in my chest was real as my heart ached with that memory. How could Sheldon have said all of that then when he knew our marriage was almost over?

I didn't feel my tears until one dripped from my cheek to my hand and I wondered how many more tears would I cry?

I pushed myself up from the chair, gathered my purse, turned off the light, then made my way to the bedroom.

And I slept in my bed, which was much more comfortable than that cot. At least for my body. The problem was, there was no place for me to rest my heart.

Chapter THIRTEEN

I'd just hung up the phone from Kym, telling her that I would drive myself to the hospital this morning. She didn't protest the way I'd expected. But then the second I rested the phone back in the cradle, it rang again.

Sure that my daughter had changed her mind, I said, "Kym, really, I'm fine. I'll see you at the hospital in a little while."

"Savannah?"

Just the sound of his voice made me feel my heartbeat. "Dr. David, did something happen to Sheldon?" I asked, wishing that I'd looked at the Caller ID first. Maybe if I'd seen the call coming from the hospital, I would've been better prepared.

"No, no. I'm sorry to worry you like that. Your husband is fine."

"Oh, my God." I sank onto our bed. "It's just that when I heard your voice...."

Even though I couldn't see him, I heard his smile when he said, "Trust me, your husband is going to be fine."

I was going to ask him how could he be so sure? But I stopped myself. He was the doctor. If anyone knew, he did. He said, "I was calling because I'm about five minutes away from you and I wanted to see if you would ride with me?"

I frowned. "So, you're not calling from the hospital?"

"No. I have late rounds this morning, so I was just on my way there. But as I was driving, I thought about you, and I'm so close, I wanted to check to see if you wanted a ride."

How did he get my telephone number? And, how did he know that he wasn't far from me?

But I answered my own questions as fast as I'd asked them. He'd gotten everything he needed from the surgery form. And that wasn't the only record the hospital had. Doctors had all kinds of access to all of our personal records.

But was this ethical? For a doctor to take those records, use them, and then just call as if we were friends? Was it ethical for a doctor to offer me a ride to the hospital?

"I'm only asking because I'm really concerned about you, Savannah," he said as if I'd spoken my questions aloud. "I'm a doctor and I'm supposed to take care of my patients in every way that I can—of course, I'm trained to take care of the body, but I never leave out the mind, and most importantly, the soul, too."

"Okay," I said slowly. "But why are you so close to me? Do you live nearby?"

"Not really. I live on the other side...of town."

"And you came over here? You went out of your way just to give me a ride?"

"An act of kindness should never be considered out of one's way." He paused. "It's all about the heart, Savannah. I'm a heart doctor." Another beat. "And the heart is my passion."

Now, I had to pause. I'd heard that before. Hadn't Dr. Bartholomew said that same thing?

But before I could ask myself or the doctor anymore questions, I felt that peace. That peace that I always felt with him. That peace that drew me in, that made me want to spend my time with him. "Okay," I said. "I was just getting ready to leave, so I'll be ready."

"I'll be there in five minutes."

In four minutes, my doorbell rang.

As I slipped my bag onto my shoulder, I took a quick glance in the mirror just to check my makeup. Sheldon may have been in Intensive Care, but that didn't mean that I shouldn't look good.

I'd worn all black today, knowing that the turtleneck and slacks made me look thinner. And, in addition to my makeup, I'd curled my hair so that the layers framed my face.

Puckering my lips, I stepped toward the door and wondered if this was how Sheldon's affair had started? Had he done an act of kindness for Ginger? Or had she done something special for him? Had it started out innocent and then innocence twisted to infidelity and betrayal?

I greeted Dr. David when I opened the door. "You didn't have to get out of your car."

His smile went away as he took in my appearance. Then, he cleared his throat and spoke. "What? I should have just honked?" He shook his head. "I would never do that. A gentleman would never do that."

Of course he wouldn't.

I wasn't surprised that he was driving a larger SUV, given his height. But the color of his vehicle—white on the outside and the interior...now all of that white surprised me. I'd figured that he would be a black car driver, to go with his tall, dark, and fine features. To go with his mystique.

He held the door open and I slid into the softest leather seats I'd ever felt. They were like butter, like melted butter, almost as if they weren't really there. Like I was sitting on a cloud. Yes, a leather cloud.

A second later, he hopped in on the other side. He put the key in the ignition and asked, "Are you strapped?"

"What?" I asked with my eyes wide.

He laughed. "Do you have your seatbelt on?"

"Oh," I said, taking an extra long breath. "I thought you were asking...."

"If you had a gun?" More laughter from him. When he finally stopped chuckling at my expense, he said, "Isn't it funny how we all see things differently based on our experiences?"

"What do you mean?"

"Well, I was talking about a seatbelt and you were thinking about a gun."

"The only time I've ever heard those words—being strapped—it's always pertained to a gun."

"That's what I mean. I meant one thing and you meant another. But that's how it often is in life—things appear to be one way, but are actually different from what we see. It's like our eyes lie."

I couldn't believe this man was saying this!

I'd heard that line before. From Theresa. Whenever she caught one her husbands. Those cheaters always tried to convince her that she hadn't seen what she saw.

Don't believe your lying eyes!

Was that something that all men said?

Dr. David had just made it official for me. My friend was right—all men were lying, cheating dogs.

Well, I knew one thing. No matter what this man said, my eyes hadn't lied. I know what I saw. And not only had I seen those panties, I'd held that strip of cloth in my hands.

"Like for instance," Dr. David said, "the sun appears to be smaller than the earth, but we know that it's not." He paused as if he were giving me time to think about that. "Or how the ocean looks flat, but the earth is round. Perception is not always reality."

Whatever! I said in my head. I knew that Dr. David wasn't talking about Sheldon and Ginger, but that's how I *perceived* it. And my perception *was* reality.

The evidence was clear. Those two were guilty!

"You understand what I'm saying, right?"

I shrugged. "I guess."

"There's no need for guessing. Just don't believe everything that you *think* you see. Our sight alone cannot produce all the facts. Sometimes we have to use our other senses, and sometimes we have to use knowledge and wisdom. And the best of times, we have to just go to God and He'll answer us deep down in our soul and tell us a truth that's different from what we see."

I did something that I never did. I did something that I thought was pure ghetto—I rolled my eyes, sucked my teeth, and if I'd had anything to say, I would've shown him my best black girl neck roll.

Dr. David and I weren't talking about the same thing, but he was still pissing me off.

But then, I took a deep breath. He didn't know that he was getting on my nerves. And I definitely didn't need to take out my situation on him.

So, I just leaned back in the softness of the seats. And allowed the peace that I always felt when I was with him to overtake me again.

But in the silence, his words screamed in my head:

Our sight alone cannot produce all the facts.

What did that mean? And could I apply it to my situation?

Right away, I tossed that thought aside. I didn't have to rely on anything else...not my other senses, not other knowledge or wisdom. Not anything.

Those thongs were plainly in front of me.

I saw them. I held them. I did everything but smell them.

Those thongs were in my husband's luggage.

Case. Closed.

Dr. David pulled in front of the hospital and turned off the car.

"You're not getting out?" I asked when he didn't park his truck.

He nodded. "I am. But I'm a gentleman, remember? I never let a woman walk too far in her heels."

I chuckled as I took a quick glance down at my boots. "Okay." I put my hand on the door handle, then paused. "You are coming up, right?" I hoped my voice didn't have the desperation in it that I felt.

This was the most bizarre thing to me. This man had just pissed me off, even though he didn't know it. Yet, I still wanted to be around him. When I was with Dr. David, it was like I was still in the valley, but there was such serenity in this place that I would consider one of the lowest of my life.

He covered my hand with his and smiled. And I held my breath. If he didn't move his hand away, I was going to faint. Right here in this man's car.

"I'll be right up after I park the car."

"I'll wait for you then."

"No. You go on up. Go on up to your husband."

Why did he have to remind me that I had a husband?

"Okay," I said. I slid out of the car and wanted to stand there and watch him drive off the way I did when Sheldon left our home.

But Dr. David didn't budge and I guessed he was waiting for me. So I walked toward the hospital's doors. I imagined him watching me, and I wished that I'd worn a pair of stilettos. Because those shoes always made a woman's stride sexy—if she knew how to do it.

And I knew how. I hadn't used it much over the years, but I knew how. Dr. David was helping me to remember that, and a whole bunch of other things.

Chapter FOURTEEN

"Mother, what took you so long?" Kym met me at the elevator.

"What's wrong? Did something happen to your father?"

"Yes! He woke up!" she said, sounding excited and annoyed at the same time.

"He's awake?" I said, although I didn't wait for her answer. I rushed down the halls, past the nurses, not even bothering to stop and say hello the way I normally did.

Behind me, Kym followed, talking all the way. "He was awake, but he's not now. I told him that you were on your way, but he only kept his eyes open for a few seconds."

"That's exactly what happened to me," I said, stepping into the room. Putting my coat and purse on the chair, I moved to the bed.

Looking down at him, there were no signs at all that he'd opened his eyes. He looked exactly the way he did when I left him last night.

"I can't believe I missed that," I whispered.

It must have been the way I sounded that made Kym soften her tone. "Well, he's going to wake up again soon. I'm sure of it." Kym took my hand and squeezed it. "And the next time, I have a feeling that he's going to stay awake for good!"

I hoped Kym was right. When Dr. David came up here, I'd ask him when he thought that would be.

Kym's cell phone buzzed, indicating that she had a text and when my daughter glanced down at her phone, she sighed.

"What's wrong?"

"It's Professor Tasker. She said that there's no way for me to get an extension on my application."

"You're not done?"

"Not yet. I have most of it completed; I just have to finish the essay."

"Well, you need to go work on it."

"But, I'd wanted to spend the day with Daddy," she whined.

"And what do you think your father would want you to do? He's so proud that you want to do this. Both of us are."

"I know, but—"

"And, I'll be here with him."

"But that's the problem. You're the one who's been pulling all the hours."

"I should, I'm his wife."

"But I feel like I'm letting you," she paused and glanced at Sheldon in the bed, "and Daddy down." When she said 'Daddy' tears welled in her eyes.

"Oh, sweetheart," I said, turning away from Sheldon and pulling her into my arms. "You have been a lifesaver for me. You've helped just because I know that I can call on you. So please don't feel that way."

She nodded. "Okay." Then, wiped her eyes. "So, I'm going to go home and finish."

"Good. Write that essay and show them just how fantastic you are."

I kissed my daughter's cheek, then sent her on her way. But before she walked out the door, she said, "Call me if you want a break or anything."

I nodded, even though we both knew that I wouldn't call her nor would I take a break.

Once I was alone, I pulled up the chair and sat at the edge of Sheldon's bed. Except for the monitor that measured his heartbeat, the room was quiet. I heard the muffled sounds of activity through the closed door, but inside this space, it was just me and Sheldon.

Truly, I wished he would wake up right now. Then, I could ask him every question and he wouldn't be able to get away. He'd have to answer me.

But of course, if he woke up this instant, I wouldn't say a word about the red-thong wearing Ginger. I wouldn't want to take the chance of being the cause of another heart attack. His body might not survive that.

So, I just sat there watching his chest move up, then down. Watching the peace that was over his face as he slept.

I reached over the rail and took his hand into both of mine. As I caressed his hand, I thought about the millions of times we'd held each other and wondered if, when he opened his eyes, we would ever do this again.

"Sheldon," I whispered his name. "What happened? How did we get here? Wasn't I good enough for you?" I paused, feeling tears rising up inside of me. It hurt so much to know that all of this love that we'd had was over—maybe.

The slight knock on the door made me snatch my hands away from Sheldon and wipe my face even though tears had yet to fall.

One of the nurses that I spoke to every morning peeked into the room. "These were just delivered for Mr. Hudson," she said, holding up a bouquet of flowers.

"Flowers?"

She nodded. "They're silk, so they're okay to have in here." Stepping further into the room, she asked, "Do you want me to put these over there?" She pointed to the table where Ginger had left her iPod.

"Yes," I said, as I pressed my legs together to stop them from shaking.

Then, the nurse glanced at Sheldon's chart and checked his heart monitor and breathing tube. I wanted to shout, 'Hurry up," but I didn't say a word. Just watched her until she walked out of the room.

Then, I dashed over to the flowers and snatched the card from the center.

Ginger had clearly lost her mind. Even though she didn't know that I knew about her and Sheldon, she had to suspect something since I had asked her to stay away. And, I hadn't called her and she'd been smart enough not to call me.

But maybe she wasn't too bright. Because she'd sent these flowers!

My hands were shaking as I read the card:

With all my love,

Candace.

Wait! What?

I had to read the card again. And then, again. And again.

Candace? Candace. Candace!

Oh, my God! I sank onto the sofa.

Candace! I never thought of her. Sheldon's new intern. I'd never met her, though I'd expected to meet her at the annual Christmas Eve luncheon that Sheldon always had for his staff.

But Sheldon had told me all about her. He couldn't stop raving about her. How she was smart, and efficient, and beautiful. Yes, I remember him saying beautiful.

I'd thought nothing of it at the time because Sheldon had never given me a single reason to feel envious or be jealous of any woman.

I was his air and his world...at least that's what he always told me.

But it seemed that there was someone new in town.

And if the red-thonged woman was Candace, that meant...I'd been wrong about Ginger!

Oh, my God!

I sat there and thought about that for a moment. And then, I shook my head. There was no way that I could do this. No way that I could just sit here and like I'd done with Ginger, wonder for days and days and days about Candace.

Taking a quick glance at Sheldon, I grabbed my coat, purse, and stomped out of the room.

"Will you be back, Mrs. Hudson?"

I paused and looked into the face of the nurse who'd just brought me the flowers. "Yes," I said. "I just have to make a quick...run."

"Well, you know we'll take care of Mr. Hudson, right?"

"I know and thank you." I took two steps away and then turned back. "You know what? I've been here for all of these days and I don't know your name. I don't know any of your names."

"I'm Keisha," she said.

"Well, thank you, Keisha. I'll be back in about an hour."

"Okay, and when you come back, I'll introduce you to all the other nurses."

"Great. And if Dr. David comes by, can you tell him that I'll be right back?"

At first, she nodded, then, she asked, "Dr. David?" But before she said anything else, a buzzer sounded. "Excuse me," she said as she rushed down the hall.

As soon as she was out of my sight, my thoughts returned to Ginger...and Candace.

How wrong I'd been! But I knew I was right now. And I was going to handle both of these things. First, I'd apologize to Ginger. And then...what was I going to do to Candace? I had no idea, but something was going down.

It wasn't until I got outside that I remembered I didn't have my car! There was no way I was going to call Kym from her apartment or Theresa from work.

And although Dr. David didn't ever seem to be too busy with other patients, I couldn't ask him for a ride.

I clicked the Internet icon on my cell, Googled taxis and hit the first number that came up. Five minutes later, a cab rolled up to the front door of Howard University Hospital.

After I gave the address to Sheldon's downtown office, I sat back and smoldered with anger. Anger at myself for not thinking it all the way through with Ginger. And anger at Candace for being the snake who had slithered into our Garden of Eden.

When the cab stopped on the corner of 12th and H Streets, I tossed a twenty to the driver and didn't even wait for him to give me change.

Inside, I tried my best to bring it down. I didn't want to walk into Sheldon's office as an angry black woman—even though that's exactly what I was.

On the 7th floor, the elevator doors parted. I stepped off and then, I stopped, stunned.

I cleared my throat and then two pairs of eyes looked back at me.

"Savannah," Ginger and Jon, Sheldon's business partner called my name at the same time, and then they dropped their hands from their embrace.

Jon stepped up to me first. "Savannah, how are you?" he asked, then pulled me into his arms, though he didn't hold me the way he'd just been holding Ginger. "How's Sheldon? Did something happen?" he asked without giving me a chance to answer.

"No, I mean...." I paused and took a breath. "I'm good and Sheldon is recovering. I thought you were in Paris."

"I just got back," he said. "Last night. I was going to come to the hospital today, but Ginger said that you only wanted family there."

I looked from Ginger, back to Jon, then back to Ginger.

"Savannah...." Ginger said, then she stopped when Jon held up his hand.

"I'll tell her, sweetheart." He put his arms around Savannah's waist. "I know you were probably a little surprised to see me and Ginger...."

I nodded.

"Well, Ginger and I are engaged."

My eyes darted between the two of them again. "Really?"

Ginger nodded and grinned like a schoolgirl. "Yes. We were trying to keep it a secret because Sheldon and Jon have such a strict policy about fraternizing in the office."

Jon shook his head. "It's our company, our rules, but you know your husband," he said. "He wanted to go strictly by the book. Didn't want us to announce it until Ginger found a new position outside of our company."

Ginger nodded. "He didn't even want me to tell you." She laughed. "I almost begged him once; I told him that he had to at least tell you!"

The text!

Have you told Savannah? At least, tell Savannah.

"But after what happened to Sheldon, we didn't want to wait a minute longer," Jon said, holding Ginger even closer. "So that's why we're going to announce it to the world!" He laughed, then kissed Ginger again as if I weren't standing there.

"Well, congratulations," I said. "To both of you."

"Thank you." Then, Ginger said, "So everything is all right with Sheldon?"

I nodded. "He's healing. He's opened his eyes a few times. Usually, he would be awake by now, but his heart specialist believed that Sheldon's heart needed a little more time. So he's been giving him something to sleep more."

"Oh. So then." Ginger stopped as if that were a full sentence.

"He really is getting better and the doctors are expecting a full recovery."

"That's terrific," Ginger said and hugged me. "Thank you for coming all the way up here to tell us. But I would've come to you."

"No, it was good for me to get out of the hospital for a little while, and...I wanted to meet Sheldon's new intern. Candace sent him flowers and I wanted to *personally* thank her."

"Candace will love that!" Ginger said. "Why don't you wait in Sheldon's office and I'll get her for you." Before she turned though, she planted another kiss on Jon and if I had any lingering doubts (which I didn't) they were all gone with the way Jon and Ginger were together. They were in love, the way Sheldon and I used to be.

Giving Jon another hug, I went to Sheldon's office and closed the door behind me. Glancing around, this seemed more like a shrine to his family than a place of business. There were pictures of me and Kym and Kyle everywhere. On his desk, on the credenza, on the book shelves. There were photos of us on vacation, enjoying the holidays, and celebrating every milestone of our children's lives.

I sat down on the leather love seat and with all these symbols of our love around me, I began to plot what I was going to say to Candace. I wanted to make sure that she understood what she'd done. I wanted her to feel my hurt and fear my anger. I wanted her to be shamed by my disgust.

I wasn't even going to ask her any questions because I was sure that she would just lie. So, I was going to tell her what I knew and then, I was going to tell her to give me one reason why I shouldn't go straight Brenda Richie on her behind.

Then, the door to Sheldon's office opened...slowly. I stood, I waited. And then, I had another moment of shock as Candace rolled in and over to me.

In her wheelchair.

"Mrs. Hudson," Candace exclaimed, clearly having no idea that she had almost entered an ambush. "I am so happy to meet you."

She was right next to me when she grabbed my hand and shook it with such enthusiasm I was afraid she might break my wrist.

She said, "I hate that we're meeting under these circumstances, but I couldn't wait to meet you because Mr. Hudson talks about you all the time." She released a soft

chuckle. "And when I say all the time, I mean it. I don't think
I've ever met a man who loved his wife so much."

It was a good thing that she kept talking because I was
speechless.

She said, "So Ginger said that Mr. Hudson is doing well."

"Yes," I said, uttering my first word. "Very well." I fell
back onto the sofa because I wasn't sure my legs could sustain
me.

"I know this has been so hard on you and your son and
daughter. How are Kym and Kyle?"

Clearly, Sheldon had shared his life with this woman.
This forty-something-year-old woman who I was sure wasn't
the object of Sheldon's affection. Not because she was in a
wheelchair—she really was a beautiful woman, Diahann
Carroll's daughter if I had to compare her to anyone. But she
was a little bigger than the size four waist that would've fit
into those thongs.

I just had to ask, "Sheldon told me that you were his
intern?"

She nodded. "I went back to college two years ago. I was
at Howard twenty years ago when I got into a car accident
that left me like this." She looked down at her legs. "For a
long time, I felt sorry for myself, I felt like crap." All I could
do was nod as she spoke because so much guilt had settled
in my throat.

She continued, "For a long time, I saw myself as a crippled person. But then, I met this doctor who told me that I couldn't rely on what I saw. He convinced me that I had to see beyond my legs and beyond these wheels, and look for the strength within my heart."

I sat up a little straighter. "This doctor? Was his name Doctor David?"

She frowned as if she were trying to remember. "I don't know. I only talked to him once. I met him at church. He was in the section for wheelchairs like I was. He said he was a heart doctor, though."

I tilted my head a little. Such a coincidence. His words sounded like Dr. David's, but my doctor could clearly walk.

She said, "So anyway, I went back to school and I'll be graduating in June."

"Good for you," I said, now understanding why Sheldon bragged on this woman so much. He had never mentioned that she was in a wheelchair, but I could see why. Once you met her, her wheelchair kind of disappeared. I saw past her legs and the wheels and in even just these few minutes, I just saw Candace.

"You have no idea how wonderful it is to meet you," I said.

She beamed. "I hope I'll get a chance to see you again soon. And, I really hope that Mr. Hudson will be home soon. Really soon."

Leaning over, I gave her a tight hug. Even though I'd just met her, I loved her already—for so many reasons.

I said goodbye, then peeked into Ginger's office and thanked her again.

"And, Ginger, if you and Jon want to come and visit Sheldon, please do."

"Thank you, Savannah. I really want to; I hated having to stay away."

More guilt filled my heart.

I hugged her, told her to tell Jon that I said goodbye, then made my way down the elevator and out of the building. I wouldn't have to call a cab this time. I just stood on the corner, held up my hand and in less than three minutes, a taxi stopped.

It wasn't until I was inside the car that I let all the thoughts I had pour down on me.

It wasn't Ginger. It wasn't Candace. If I had been wrong about those two, could I be wrong about everything else?

But I saw the thong! I held the thong!

It wasn't Ginger. It wasn't Candace. But those panties belonged to someone.

I just had to find a way to figure out who the mystery woman really was.

Chapter FIFTEEN

I spent the evening alone with Sheldon. That was what I really wanted to do. So, I called to check on Kym and told her to stay home and not to leave her apartment until she finished.

Then, I called Theresa.

"You don't have to come up here tonight," I said.

"Why not? Are you going home?"

"No, I'm going to stay up here. But I want some time alone with Sheldon. Just me and him."

"Is he awake?"

"No, but I want to talk to him. With just the two of us in the room."

She paused for a moment, then said, "*Chica*, that is so romantic." She sighed. "One day...I'm telling you one day, *Mami*, I will have a love just like that. I want a love like yours."

Of course, I said nothing except goodbye. Because when the time came and I had to tell Theresa the truth, I wouldn't be bursting her bubble, I'd be blowing it up. Theresa might never recover once she heard this news.

And so I sat alone in the room. Just staring at my husband as nurses came and went. I guess somewhere in the back of my mind, I was waiting for Dr. David, too.

But he never came, although I suspected that he'd checked on Sheldon while I was at Sheldon's office.

So I just sat, and stared and thought until I exhausted myself. It was well after ten when I called a cab and took the ten-minute ride home.

But even though I was aching-bones-tired, I couldn't sleep. No matter how many times I shifted on the sheets or tucked the pillow beneath my neck—I couldn't find that sweet spot for sleep.

"Lord, please," I finally whispered. "Please let me rest."

That must have been the true desire of my heart because my eyelids finally were too heavy for me to hold open.

So I closed my eyes.

And I slept.

And I dreamed....

I was floating, floating, floating until I stopped in a space with dim lights that twinkled above, below and to each side of me. There was music, sweet music, from a saxophone, I believe, though I didn't see anyone playing. I just heard music that was like nothing I'd ever heard before. Each note touched me, like really physically touched me somewhere in my soul.

And the song that played—I wasn't familiar with it, but I knew it was romantic. I knew it was a love song. Probably the most romantic love song that had ever been written.

Where am I? I wondered inside my head.

"You're here. With me."

I didn't see him, not at first. But I wasn't afraid because I heard him. And his voice, though deep, was almost as sweet as the music.

Then, he stepped into my view. Wearing a suit that had to have been painted onto his skin. And the fragrance he wore—it was the cologne that he always wore.

"You look beautiful," Dr. David said as he floated toward me.

I glanced down to check out my dress, but I didn't see anything. Not that I was naked; that part of me was all a blur. Except for my heart. I saw my heart, beating, against the beautiful blackness of the space.

He said, "Your heart beats so beautifully."

His words made me beam.

"You were made with a heart to love. You were made with a heart that believes."

That made me frown. Believe in what?

"Not what, but whom," he said as if I'd spoken. "You were made with a heart to believe in others."

Okay, I thought, not really sure of what he meant.

Then, he added, "You have a heart that was made to love and believe in your husband."

What? I would never believe in Sheldon! And I knew it might take some time, but I was going to erase all of the love I had for him, too.

Again, he spoke, as if I'd spoken aloud. "You have to believe in your husband in order to experience this miracle."

Why should I ever believe in Sheldon again?

"Believe in him because you love him."

I shook my head. Not for much longer.

"You're just thinking that because you've been hurt," he said, continuing the conversation with me even though I hadn't spoken a single word aloud. "But you brought this pain on yourself."

"What?" Now the words came out of me. "I brought on this pain? It's my fault that Sheldon had an affair?"

"Yes."

"How am I responsible? I was the good wife; I was at home making sure that my man came home to a comfortable place, a wonderful meal, and a loving wife all the time. I lived to make his life better. I made Sheldon better. So, I'm not going to take responsibility because he couldn't keep it in his pants."

"But you have to take responsibility...for your thoughts."

There were all kinds of names that I wanted to call Dr David, but none of them came to mind. "Thoughts cannot make a person cheat."

"Oh, yes!" he said. "Yes, they can. You thought Sheldon's whole affair. Every sin he's committed, you thought about. Every woman he's been with was hand-picked by your thoughts. You even. . ."

"It's not my fault."

"It is."

The more I said it wasn't, the more he said it was.

We went on and on and I couldn't get him to stop. Until I leaned forward. And held his face between my hands. And pressed my lips against his. Soft wonderful lips. And a soft wonderful kiss.

I tried to press my body against his, but then, my eyes popped open.

I looked around the darkened room. There were no glittering lights, no table floating in the clouds and no Dr. David.

But then, with my fingertips, I felt my lips. And it felt like his lips were still there.

Had that been a dream?

It didn't feel like one.

Slowly, I laid my head back down. But I didn't fall asleep. And, I didn't even pray for sleep. This time, I wanted to keep my eyes open. This time, all I wanted to do was think about that kiss.

Chapter SIXTEEN

I felt so guilty.

Because I couldn't stop thinking about that kiss. But it had just been a dream; I hadn't really kissed Dr. David.

So, as I sat here with Sheldon, why did I feel so guilty?

Glancing at the clock, I couldn't believe that almost three hours had passed since I arrived and it was just now approaching ten in the morning.

I had rolled out of bed early, since I couldn't sleep anyway. And had driven to the hospital, just as it had started to snow. At least that was a good thing, if it really stormed, I would be here already. And, I could stay here, if I had to.

So, I had come here and just sat, and hoped and prayed that Sheldon would open his eyes.

But so far this morning, none of that had happened. I'd sat here with nothing but my thoughts.

Looking at him now, it was hard for me to imagine Sheldon with Ginger, Candace or any other woman. I just couldn't see it.

I pushed that wishful hope aside, though. I wasn't the first wife who'd been cheated on who felt that way. We all thought we'd married Supermen until we discovered that they were just mere men.

Lord, I so wanted all of these thoughts to end. I wanted no more conjecture in my head, no more speculation in my heart. All I wanted was the truth. To know the truth spoken from Sheldon's lips.

Standing up, I leaned on the bedrail, looking down at Sheldon for a moment. And I thought—what would happen if I just shook him awake and made him answer me?

Though I wanted to do that, of course, I wouldn't. It hadn't worked out so well the last time I put my hands on him.

I needed some kind of solution, though. Four full days and counting. How much more of this would I be able to take?

Moving closer to my husband, I whispered, "Sheldon, talk to me. Please. Wake up and talk to me."

Nothing.

"Sheldon?"

More nothing.

I straightened my back to stand, but then, Sheldon's eyelids fluttered.

"Sheldon!" I said, leaning close to him once again.

His eyes opened wide. Wider this time than before.

"Sheldon," I said, wondering if he heard me.

He squinted just a bit, as if he were trying to focus. And then, his head turned slightly so that his eyes were looking straight into mine.

"Sheldon!"

He parted his lips. Just like he did before. He was straining, struggling to speak. He wanted to tell me something.

He must have remembered how he got here. He must have remembered what we were talking about. He wanted to tell me what I needed to know.

"What is it, Sheldon? What is it?"

He swallowed hard, like he was aware. Like he was ready to tell me the truth.

Looking straight into my eyes, he said, "Miranda."

"What?"

"Miranda," he said so clearly, this time.

Then, his eyes closed once again.

"Sheldon!" I shouted, once again thinking about shaking him.

How could he do this to me? How could he just wake up and call me by someone else's name...his mistress's name.

Miranda.

I wanted to move away, but I couldn't. My legs weren't strong enough. And my own heart was too weak now. I couldn't even feel it beating.

Miranda.

For minutes upon minutes, hours upon hours, days upon days, I'd been waiting for answers. Finally, I had the most important one.

Miranda.

But, who was Miranda?

I scrolled through the contact list in my mind for someone named Miranda.

His office? No. At church? No. We didn't even have a neighbor named Miranda.

So, his mistress was someone I didn't know, a woman I'd never met. Maybe she was a flight attendant who accompanied Sheldon on his cross country trips. Or maybe she was a business woman herself who'd met Sheldon at the Chamber of Commerce.

I shook my head. There was no doubt I'd be crazy-silly trying to figure out where this woman came from.

Miranda.

Miranda.

Miranda.

My tears came when the last chorus of her name played in my mind. I had a thong and a name. It was official...it was really over.

I thought that I couldn't hurt anymore than I'd been hurting, but I was wrong. When I thought it was Ginger or Candace, my heart ached, but not as much as when the name had come straight from Sheldon rather than from my mind.

Grabbing my purse, I rushed from the room. I didn't even pause at the Nurses' station, not even when I heard one of the women call out to me.

In the elevator, I kept my head down, wanting to hide my tears. Though I was in a hospital—no one would really notice me crying. Still, I covered my eyes and ran from the building.

But then, I stepped outside and the frigid temperature wrapped itself around me. Not only that, it was snowing. Big flakes. Storm Watch 2014.

Dang! I had left my coat in Sheldon's room.

So now I was cold and heartbroken.

It didn't matter. I wasn't going back up there. I was never going to see Sheldon Hudson again—except in court.

Dashing to my car, I jumped inside, locked the door and trembled from the cold and from the misery in my heart. I turned on the ignition, switched the heat to high, and then, I let my tears fall and my sobs fill the car.

The pain that surrounded my heart was like something that I'd never felt before. And, it felt like a pain that would never end.

If I'd known that it was going to hurt this much, I would've never asked the questions. Because I didn't really need to know these answers. It would have been so much better for me if I hadn't found that thong. It would've been fine if Sheldon had just kept on cheating and cheating and cheating. And I would have been oblivious to it all and would've been able to continue living my perfect life.

I sobbed and I sobbed and I sobbed until there were no tears left in me. I sobbed until I made a decision and put together a plan.

I was going home. And I would pack. And I would leave. I had no idea where I was going, but I wouldn't be in our townhouse when Sheldon was released from the hospital.

I'd fulfilled my wifely duties, every single one of them. Now it was time for me to step aside because I would never be anyone's door mat. Let the thong-wearing home-wrecking Miranda step in. Let Sheldon see that no one would ever take care of him the way that I did.

Finally, I eased out of the parking space knowing that the streets became slick quickly, especially with how thick the snow was. I needed to be careful, but my mind was so consumed. I had to take my thoughts away, so I turned on the radio.

Hang all the mistletoe
I wanna get to know you better...
This Christmas.

I released one long painful howl. I twisted the knob for the radio so hard, that for a moment, I thought I broke it.

Why did they have to play my favorite Christmas song right at that moment? My favorite and Sheldon's favorite.

I was crying so hard that I really needed to pull over. But I just wanted to get home. So that I could pack and I could leave.

The snow was falling so hard now, that it looked like a white sheet was in front of me. I had to stop crying, I needed to if I was going to make it home safely. But I couldn't stop. Because everywhere I looked, there was Sheldon.

He was at the Verizon Center where we'd gone to so many Wizards games. And he was at the Red Velvet Cupcakery where he often surprised me with my favorite cupcakes. And there was the mall that stretched from the U.S. Capitol to the Lincoln Memorial, where Sheldon and I had run, practicing for the Marine Corps marathon, though our commitment to run had only lasted a week.

My tears were as thick as the snow. Maybe that was why when my car hit a slick spot, I didn't know what to do because I could hardly see.

I screamed as the car jerked first to the left, then to the right, sliding for several feet, until I heard the BOOM over my screams. I jolted forward, then back before the car finally came to a stop.

My heart was pounding, pounding, pounding.

I checked to see if I was still breathing. And then next to see if I could move—my arms, my legs.

My neck was a little sore, but everything seemed to be in place—and still working.

I thanked God!

I was alive. But now, what was I supposed to do. I reached for my cell phone to call...Sheldon. I sighed. I was going to have to start being a big girl now, anyway. This was a good time to start.

So where to start? We had Triple A, I was sure. I pulled out my wallet, and then, jumped as someone knocked on my window.

The windows were already clouding up from the snow, but I could see him.

I rolled down the window. "Dr. David, what...."

"I was on my way to the hospital," he explained before I completely asked the question. "I didn't want to drive because of the storm, so I took a cab, but as we were turning, I saw your car."

"I skidded," I said.

He moved a couple of feet to the front of the car. "And you blew out a tire."

"I was just about to call for help."

"Okay," he said. "Get out and get in the back seat. I'll keep you warm while we wait for the tow truck."

"Keep me warm?"

"You don't have your coat, do you?"

"How did you...."

"Because you only have on that sweater. And it's freezing out here." He rubbed his gloved hands together. "Come on."

"But, I can turn on the heat."

He shook his head. "It's not going to work. Your car is not going to start."

Just because I didn't trust men anymore, I turned the key in the ignition.

Nothing.

I looked up at Dr. David and frowned.

He looked down at me and shrugged.

I had no idea what happened, but I was getting cold already. So, I jumped from the front seat into the back. And by the time Dr. David slid in next to me, he'd taken off his coat and used it as a blanket to cover both of us.

Still, I shivered. But I wasn't so sure that it was from the cold.

He put his arm around my shoulders and I had no choice but to kind of lay my head on his chest.

"Are you warm enough?"

He had no idea. "Yes," I said. "Thank you."

"Give me your phone so that I can call for emergency road service."

"I can do it," I said.

"No, let me take care of you, let me take care of this."

"Okay. Do you have a number?"

He nodded. "I always know who to call."

Even as he made the call, we stayed close. The heat of him didn't just keep me warm; he was setting me on fire.

When he hung up from the call, he wrapped his arms round me once again and I closed my eyes. I imagined that Dr. David was the man that I loved, that he was the man who loved me back. I imagined that he would never cheat on me.

"You know, Savannah, things are not always as they seem."

I hoped he wasn't going to give me another one of those don't-believe-your-lying-eyes lectures.

"Sometimes, you have to search deep in your heart to know the truth. And know that no matter what, God is talking to you. God's got you."

I paused for a moment, taking in his words. "And sometimes, you talk like you know me. Like you know the things that are going on in my life."

"I know enough." With his forefinger and thumb, he turned my chin until I had to shift and was looking up at him. "I can see it in your eyes. Your eyes have been sad from the moment I've met you."

"Well, my husband did have a heart attack."

He shook his head. "Your sadness goes beyond that. In your heart, you know that he will be all right. But your heart hasn't told you yet that you will be fine, too."

We were so close as we sat there, looking into each other's eyes. And his lips...they were right there in front of me.

All I wanted to do was kiss him. I wanted to finish wha
I'd started in my dream. Because if I kissed him, then, he'
kiss me. And I would know for sure that my heart woul
definitely be fine.

The seconds ticked by. My eyes on him, his, on me
And my heart did another one of those little flutter beats
Something that had only happened with Sheldon.

That was what made me move forward, but just as I did
a car horn blaring, startling me. I sat up; it was difficult to se
through the window. The snow was falling in blankets now.

"Great, they're here," Dr. David said.

"Already?" No tow truck service *ever* came that fast
Especially not in this weather with so many emergencies on
the road.

But here they were. Messing up my flow.

Dr. David jumped out of the car. "Stay here," he said a
he headed straight to the tow truck driver.

From inside the car, I watched him as much as I could.
had almost done it. Something that I'd never done before. I'c
almost kissed another man.

And the anticipation felt so good. I couldn't imagine
what the real kiss—and more—would be like.

With a sigh, I smiled.

Dr. David and I were meant to be. The universe had tc
know that or why was he always in my presence? Why was

e always there right when I needed him? It was almost like
e were in love—already.

That was when I made another decision. I didn't know
when and I didn't know how. But I was going to finish what
'd just tried to start.

Dr. David and I would be together. And really, I could
hank Sheldon for that.

Chapter
SEVENTEEN

W'ed had to squeeze into the front seat with the tow truck driver who was kind enough to give us a ride to my house.

"You don't want to be trying to wait for a cab out here," he said.

So, I'd practically sat on Dr. David's lap and the driver drove the two miles to my home. But it seemed that the emergency workers couldn't keep up with the snow; what would normally take five minutes, took us twenty five as even the tow truck slipped and skidded a couple of times.

Any other time, I would've been scared and praying to make it home. But even though I couldn't wait to get home, I had no fear. I never did when I was with Dr. David.

Instead, I used the minutes to imagine what my life would be like from now on. I would be a doctor's wife, because I wasn't built to be anyone's girlfriend. So after a respectful courtship, we'd be married.

And we'd live...wherever he wanted. And we'd have passion, real passion. I'd really pay attention this time, though. I'd pay attention to what turned him on. Maybe I'd even find a way to wear a thong or two.

But first, there would be tonight. Because there would be no way for Dr. David to get to the hospital now. Cabs wouldn't be on the roads, this was too unsafe. So, he'd be stranded at my house. With me.

I wondered if I should cook something for him first. Or should we make love and then eat. I really didn't know how these things were supposed to go. I'd just have to let it play out naturally.

When we arrived, I'd show him where the wood was out on the deck so that he could start the fire. While he was doing that, I'd change into something more comfortable, of course.

And then, I'd play music. I didn't know what, but I needed something like the music that was in my dream. A tune that was perfect, one that we would always remember.

It would become our song.

I was stuffed inside a tow truck in the middle of a storm, but I was so giddy. I'd been the good girl, the nice girl all my life. But now, I was going to show Dr. David the naughty side of nice.

"Okay, here we are," the driver said.

"Thank you so much," Dr. David and I said together.

And then we smiled at each other. Our relationship wa already simpatico.

I slid off Dr. David's lap, but then as we rushed to my front door, I shook and stopped. Was I really going to do this?

Yes! I told myself. I wanted to, I *had* to.

It took me a couple of moments for my hand to steady enough for me to put the key in the door. But finally i opened, I stepped in and he stood outside.

"Come in," I motioned. "It's too cold to stand out here Plus it will take a cab a long time in this weather."

"Oh no, I'm fine, I have a way to get to the hospital."

"What are you talking about?"

"I have a friend who doesn't live too far from here. I jus wanted to make sure you got home safely. So, my mission is accomplished."

"But how many blocks away is your friend? You'll freeze, I said aloud, though those weren't the words I wanted to say I wanted to scream that he couldn't go because this was ou time. When would we have another time?

"Trust me, I won't freeze. This type weather doesn't scare me at all."

I was trying to think, think, think. How could I get him to stay?

Maybe I needed to stop with all the games. Maybe I needed to come right out and tell him what I wanted.

"I really want you to stay," I said with all kinds of emotions in my voice. I wasn't pretending. My heart was aching for this man.

"It's been a hard couple of days for me," I continued. "And I just don't want...please come in and stay awhile."

He shook his head and in that movement, I felt rejection.

He didn't want me. Sheldon didn't want me. What was happening?

"I need you," I practically begged.

His eyes were still bright, but there was a bit of sadness that I saw. Or was it pity? He said, "You don't need me, Savannah. All you need is inside of you."

He took one step back, but I reached for him, grabbed his lapel and pulled him close until my lips were upon his.

When he didn't push me away, I became bold. And parted my lips. But he didn't part his. The only move he made was to break our lips apart.

In an instant, my eyes were filled with tears. Still, I pleaded, but not with words. From the moment I'd met him, it seemed that this man knew my thoughts and I prayed that he would know them now.

He didn't say anything though, just shook his head. We stared at each other for long moments that felt like minutes, and then, he broke the silence.

"I have a gift for you," he said. With one hand, he reached into his pocket and with the other, he reached for mine.

I inhaled. Maybe if he touched me, he would really fee
me. And he'd know how much I wanted him.

But all he did was place what felt like a small cold ston
in my hand, then he closed my hand before I could see wha
he'd given me.

"I was going to give this to you tomorrow, but I think yo
need this tonight."

My fist was still closed when he leaned forward an
pressed his lips against my forehead.

Please, God. Please, God. Please, God.

Don't let this man walk out on me.

But my prayers didn't work. Because Dr. David sti
stepped back. And he still walked away. And he didn't eve
look back.

I watched him until his black overcoat faded into th
white of the snow. Only then did I close the door. I couldn'
even move. I just leaned against the door and cried. But nov
my tears weren't for what I'd lost with Sheldon. Now, I crie
because I'd lost Dr. David before I even had a chance to hav
him.

Finally, I took two steps away before I remembered th
gift. There was nothing that Dr. David could give me to mak
up for what he'd just taken away. But still, I opened my hand

It was a brown-skinned angel painted on a stone with
wide wings, a bright smile...and its face. It almost looked lik
Dr. David.

What an odd gift. Had he had his face painted on the face of an angel?

Maybe he did. Maybe he knew that's what he'd been to me.

An angel.

At least until tonight.

Chapter
EIGHTEEN

It was the night before Christmas and I was afraid to close my eyes. Because whenever I did the voices came. There were all kinds of voices: men, women, young, old, high, low. But they sang in unison.

Nobody wants you! Nobody will ever want you!

I wanted to scream to make the voices stop. But then how could I stop the truth?

So in the middle of the night I did something that I hadn't really done since this whole ordeal began; I rolled out of bed and got down on my knees. With tears in my eyes, talked to God.

"Dear, Lord. I need relief. And I know that I can only get it from you. Please, Father. Just let me rest. Take these voices from my head. And please take away all this hurt in my heart.

"I know there's nothing that can be done about my marriage because I refuse to stay with a man who doesn't vant me. A man who, in his first moments of consciousness, utters his mistress's name instead of mine."

I sobbed and wiped my tears with the duvet that covered the bed.

"All of that hurts so much, God, but I know you will be with me through this process, through the separation and divorce. But tonight, Lord, I just want to sleep. I just want to rest...."

I was tempted to ask God one more time—why? But didn't. Because I was so tired of His answer that didn't answer a thing.

Still, I stayed on my knees for a few minutes longer, before I pushed myself up and back into bed. But before I laid my head and heart down, I saw the gleaming smile. From the angel that I'd rested on my nightstand.

I picked it up and even in the darkness, I could see the intricate features. This really was a beautiful piece.

I closed my fist around it, remembering the way that Dr. David had given it to me. Then, I scooted down and pulled the duvet up to my chin.

And with the angel in my hand and the prayers still flowing from my heart, I slept.

Chapter NINETEEN

The ringing of the telephone awakened me. But sinc
it felt like I'd just closed my eyes, I didn't open them
I just patted my hand around on the nightstand until I fel
the phone.

"Hello." I sounded like there was cotton in my mouth.

"Mother, where are you?"

I pushed myself up. "You just called me on our hom
number. You know where I am."

"What I meant was why aren't you here? It's Christmas
And it's almost ten. Were you still in bed?"

"I couldn't sleep last night."

"Oh. I'm sorry. Maybe I need to start staying with you
Until Daddy comes home."

"No, that's okay, sweetheart."

"Well, you're up now. How fast can you get here?"

How was I going to tell my daughter that I never planned
to go back to the hospital? Because her father was in love

with someone else. Because in a few days I wouldn't even be living in this house.

"Mother?"

"I'm here, sweetheart. Let me take a shower and I'll call you back."

"Okay, but hurry up. I'm praying for a Christmas miracle," she said with all kinds of hope in her voice.

Hanging up, I was grateful that I had a few more minutes before I'd have to tell my daughter the truth.

There was so much to think about and I had to tell Kym and Kyle what was going on in the right way. Because while I didn't want to have anything to do with Sheldon, I really didn't want to affect his relationship with our children.

Not that I could ever do anything to separate Kym from Sheldon. But Kyle? My son would hurt because I hurt. I was going to have to figure this out.

Maybe what I needed to do was call Theresa. Yes, that's what I would do. I would shower, have tea, and call Theresa before she headed to the hospital. I'd tell her the news about me and Sheldon divorcing. She'd help me figure out how to tell the children.

Pushing myself from bed, I started with the first part of the plan.

Inside of the shower, I let all the thoughts of the past five days scroll through my mind: from finding those panties, to finally hearing her name. From meeting Dr. David, to being rejected by him last night.

That part was probably the only good thing that happened to me. In the light of this day, I didn't need to be in a relationship with another man. Not yet.

Dr. David had been right. And I hoped that I'd get the chance to tell him. Since I wouldn't be returning to the hospital, I wouldn't see him there. But, I'd call him. And thank him for everything. And even ask him if we could be friends.

I would certainly need a friend like Dr. David.

Turning off the shower, I stepped out. Step one of the plan done. Now, onto step two.

As I grabbed the towel, the telephone rang. Of course it would. But I didn't rush to answer it. It would go to voicemail. So, I finished my routine: brushed my teeth, scrubbed my face, and lotioned up before I stepped into the bedroom.

This was good. I was breathing, walking around, taking care of myself on this first unofficial day of my life as a single woman.

It was time for tea, but I paused, and decided to check my voicemail. I was sure the call had come from Theresa and I needed to let her know to meet me here, rather than at the hospital.

But still, I needed to check my voicemail in case the call had come from Kyle. Or maybe even...Dr. David.

Sitting on the edge of the bed, I dialed in for my messages. There was only one:

"Sheldon Hudson?"

I frowned at the sound of the woman's voice.

"I think you have something of mine."

My frown deepened as the woman giggled.

"Call me. My number is 202-555-3377."

I laid down the phone because I needed every bit of energy to breath.

Miranda had the nerve to call my home?

Oh! No!

I picked up the phone and tortured myself by listening to the message again, only to get the number. Then, I imagined that each time I pressed a key, I was punching that woman's face.

I wasn't the kind of wife who was going to just blame the other woman. Sheldon was the one who had exchanged vows with me, so he was most accountable.

But men wouldn't be able to cheat if women stuck together. Women wouldn't be foes if we all knew how to be friends—even with women we didn't know.

But clearly, Miranda didn't share any of these values, any of these morals that I treasured. Because if she believed these things, she would have never cheated with my husband.

And she didn't have brains either. Because if she had a brain cell or two, she would have never called my home.

But then I paused. Maybe Sheldon hadn't told her he was married. Maybe I'd married a cheat and a *liar.*

My chest hurt, that's how hard my heart was banging, feeling like it was trying to burst out. But I ignored the pain as the phone rang.

And then:

"Hello."

It was her, but I still said, "May I speak with Miranda, please?"

"I'm sorry, but there's no one here by that name."

Oh, really? She was going to play that game?

"I know who you are, you just called my house. You just left a message for my husband."

Now what was she going to say?

"Oh, Mrs. Hudson?"

"Yes," is what I said, but I wanted to say, "You know who this is heifer; don't play with me."

"I'm sorry," she said, surprising me by beginning with an apology. I just got confused when you asked for Miranda. My name is Beth-Ann."

I blinked. "Beth-Ann?" Now, I was the one who was confused. How many women did Sheldon have?

"Yes, didn't I leave my name?" She giggled again and I wondered how old was this...girl. "I always do that. I try to do so many things at one time. But anyway, I was calling because I have something that belongs to your husband."

Who was this woman?

She said, "Mr. Hudson and I must've been on the same lane last Friday because I have a suitcase that has his name n it. And I'm hoping and wishing that he has mine."

"What?"

"I have his suitcase and I didn't notice it until last night ecause when I got back from my trip on my red eye on aturday, I left right away for a trip to New York. I travel for ny job, so I always have two suitcases packed and I just got ack last night...."

It took a few seconds for her words to compute, but I lropped the phone and dashed into the closet where I'd hrown Sheldon's suitcase.

Could it be?

I couldn't get the suitcase unzipped quickly enough. Flipping back the top, I tossed out the clothes: thongs, bras, nighties—did this woman wear regular street clothes?

But right now, I didn't care.

This wasn't Sheldon's suitcase! Those were Beth-Ann's thongs.

I ran back and picked up the phone from where I dropped t.

Beth-Ann was still talking, "...And so that airline thought It would be good for me to first see if Mr. Hudson had my luggage, and if he didn't, then, they'd put a trace on mine."

"No, we have it!" I said, sounding so happy for her.

"Oh, that's great! Some of my favorite things are packed in that bag." She giggled. "I took a side trip while I was in Los Angeles to see my boyfriend," she said, perfectly content to share her business with a stranger.

But if she'd gone through Sheldon's bag the way I'd just gone through hers, we were all a little closer than strangers now.

"So, I know it's Christmas, but if it's not too much of a bother, I'd like to get my things."

"Of course," I said. "I have something I have to do but can we meet later today?"

"That would be wonderful. Just call me and we can arrange it. Merry Christmas," she sang before she hung up.

Even after Beth-Ann was gone from the phone, I still stood there for a minute, staring.

So many thoughts swirled through my mind. If only I had given Sheldon a chance to explain. He would've gone straight to the suitcase and proven that he had no idea about those panties.

Oh, my God!

I had to get to the hospital! I had to see my husband.

My husband!

I squealed as every bit of happiness and love that I'd felt for Sheldon all of these years poured back into me.

I couldn't wait to see him.

But wait—I didn't have my car.

The phone was still in my hand and I dialed as fast as I could.

"*Feliz Navidad!*" Theresa answered. "You good, *Chica*?"

"I'm better than good. But I need a ride to the hospital. And I need it fast. How quickly can you get to me?"

"How quickly do you need me?"

"Now."

"I'll be there in ten minutes after now."

That wasn't even that funny. But I laughed. Laughed like I had never laughed before. I hung up the phone and then, I saw it.

The angel that I'd slept with last night. It was resting on the pillow.

I lifted it, and held it in the palm of my hand like I did last night and I looked up toward the heavens. And the revelation was almost instant.

I asked God my question again, only this time, I switched it around a bit. I asked the basic question, the one that I should have asked first.

"Lord, did Sheldon cheat on me?"

No.

I'd been asking the wrong question! I had assumed a fact that wasn't real, so God couldn't even answer what I'd been asking. My perception wasn't reality—just like Dr. David said.

Dr. David. I squeezed the angel in my hand and I thanked God for everything.

Chapter
TWENTY

C an't you drive any faster?" I asked Theresa.

"What is wrong with you?"

"I have to get to my husband."

"I get that, but all of this snow on the road. Don't yo want to get there in one piece?"

Of course I did. But I couldn't wait to see Sheldon. couldn't wait to see him, to kiss him, to hold his hand. An most importantly to pray for him.

Sheldon needed me.

And I so wanted him.

It took everything in me not to have Theresa just drop m off at the front door. But she parked and I walked with her.. or rather, she ran with me. All the way to Sheldon's room.

I busted through the door.

"Hey, Mother," Kym said as she came from Sheldon' bedside and hugged me. "I was hoping that you would ge here."

"Why? Did your father wake up again?"

"No, not yet. But you know how much I hate leaving him alone."

"Oh, okay. You have to do something?"

She glanced at Theresa. "Well, yeah. A little something. But I'll be right back. Aunt Resa, can you go with me?"

Right away, I could tell that they were up to something, but I didn't care. My eyes, my thoughts were only on my husband.

I wasn't even quite sure when Kym and Theresa left the room since I was already at his bedside. And, I was looking down at the love of my life.

I kissed his forehead and then I held his hand in mine.

"Sheldon, I'm so sorry," I whispered to him. "How could I ever think that you were involved with anyone else?"

That was when it hit me—there was still that name—Miranda. But after all of the conclusions I'd jumped to, I was going to push that aside. God would reveal it when I needed to know.

What I knew now was that my husband was the man that I always thought he was.

I knew that from the bottom of my...healed heart.

I stood there, holding Sheldon and time just passed. I didn't care, I just held him, until my legs got tired. But I didn't want to move away. I wanted to be holding his hand when he woke up.

There was a soft knock on the door and one of the nurse
stepped inside. "I just have to check Mr. Hudson," she said.

So, I backed away and sat on the sofa and kept my eye
on Sheldon. My heart was filled with all the words I wante
to tell him. My mind was filled with all of the ways that I wa
going to make this up to him.

I leaned back on the sofa and tucked my feet beneath me
Since the nurse was there, I decided that it wouldn't hurt to
rest for a moment. I was still so tired. So, I close my eyes..
even for just for a minute....

"Mrs. Hudson. Mrs. Hudson."

I squeezed my eyes together before I opened them.

And, I looked into the eyes of...what was his name? D
Bartholomew.

"Mrs. Hudson. Your husband wants to speak to you."

There were so many thoughts going through my head
Like what was this doctor doing here? I hadn't seen him
since Sheldon's surgery.

But then, I shot straight up on the sofa. "What did you
say?"

He grinned. "Your husband wants...."

I didn't even let him finish. I popped up and leapt to
Sheldon's bed. I'm telling you, my feet never hit the ground.

And there he was, eyes open, he was even sitting up just
a little.

"Hey, baby," I said with tears rolling down my cheeks.

"Don't cry," he kind of croaked.

And that only made me cry more.

His arm jerked a little as he lifted it and with one of his gentle thumbs, he wiped my tears away.

"It's just that I'm so happy. You're going to be all right."

"Yes, I am. And I'm glad," he said. "Because I love you so much."

"And I love you. You have no idea."

I leaned over for a gentle kiss. And then I heard the squeal.

"Daddy!" Kym rushed into the room.

And she wasn't alone. She was with Theresa...and Kyle.

"Son!" I pulled him into my arms. "What are you doing here?"

"I know you said that Dad was going to be all right, but I had to be home. For Christmas." Then, he glanced over at his father. "Hey, Dad." He almost had to push his sister aside to give Sheldon a hug. "Looks like I got back just in time."

Sheldon nodded. "You said Christmas? Is it Christmas?"

"Yes," Kym said, nudging Kyle away so that she could be closest to Sheldon. "And you're the best Christmas gift ever."

I glanced at my friend who stood by the door grinning. Waving her over, I said, "Come on over, you know Sheldon wants to see you."

"It's just all so beautiful," Theresa said fanning her eye as she held back tears. And that was something because m friend was so jaded, she never cried.

I stepped aside, so she could give her own greeting t Sheldon.

"*¿Qué te tomó tanto tiempo para llegar bien.*"

"What did you say?"

"I asked him what took him so long?"

We all laughed.

I'd forgotten that Dr. Bartholomew was in the room, unti he said, "I think you're well enough to check out tomorrow.

Kym clapped her hands. "See? I knew it. This is . Christmas miracle!"

"He's all right, Doctor? I mean, I want him home, bu I want him well, first." I took his hand and when Sheldor wrapped his fingers around mine, I decided then that I woulc never let him go.

"He's going to need to take it easy and we'll be giving him a full set of instructions, including what his diet has tc be. But he'll be fine to go."

I released Sheldon's hand for just a moment because there was something else that I had to do. Pulling the doctor into ; hug, I said, "Thank you so much. Thank you so for giving me my husband back."

He nodded and when he stepped back, I asked, "Is there any way for you to page Dr. David? I'd love to introduce him to everybody while we're all here."

"Dr. David?"

"Yes, the doctor who's been taking care of Sheldon."

"I've been taking care of your husband," he said as face unched up into a mound of creases. "And I don't know...any)r. David on staff."

"The heart specialist. Dr. David. He's been here with me very day."

"Is David his first name or his last?"

"It's his...I don't know," I said. Now I was the one onfused.

"There's a lot of noise, or should I say joy coming from iis room," the nurse who'd been in the room with me this iorning said.

"Well, Miranda, it looks like Mr. Hudson is on his way to full recovery," Dr. Bartholomew said.

Miranda!

"I've been talking to you," Miranda said to Sheldon.

This nurse had been in front of me the whole time and I'd ever asked her name.

"I think I heard you," Sheldon said.

"Well, I never stopped talking, except when your wife vas here. I figured you'd rather hear her voice than mine." he laughed. "Welcome back. And Merry Christmas."

"Merry Christmas," we all said together.

Now, all of my questions had been answered.

Except—where was Dr. David?

"Daddy, what's this?" Kym said, pulling something from the side of Sheldon's pillow.

"I don't know," Sheldon said, sounding as if he were still a little groggy.

She held it up and I gasped. It was an angel. A matching angel. The angel that Dr. David had given to me.

"It's really pretty," Kym said as she handed the angel to Sheldon.

"Well, I don't know who put it there, but I feel like I've had angels watching over me."

And that was when I got it.

While my family stood all around Sheldon, I stepped back just a little. Because I had to give thanks.

I still wasn't sure that I believed it all. I mean, I had never believed in angels. But now, after this...it would explain so much.

As more laughter filled the room, I raised my eyes heavenward.

"Baby," my husband's voice sounded like a frog, "what are you doing all the way over there?" He held out his hand and Theresa and Kyle stepped aside so that I could be close to my husband. I took his hand.

"I love you, Savannah Hudson," Sheldon said.

My voice trembled as I said, "I love you, Sheldon Judson." I leaned over and held onto the man that I knew God had made just for me.

Yes.

Thank you, Lord, I said inside. Thank you for Sheldon Judson and for the angels that walk among us.